D0831356

DIANA PALMER

Storm Over the Lake

Silhouette Books

Published by Silhouette Books

America's Publisher of Contemporary Romance

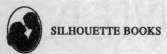

SILHOUETTE BOOKS

ISBN 0-373-63179-0

STORM OVER THE LAKE

First published in North America as a MacFadden Romance by Kim Publishing Corporation.

Visit Silhouette at www.eHarlequin.com

Printed in U.S.A.

One

There was a sense of foreboding in the morning. Dana Meredith crossed out her second try at a lead for the news-feature she was writing about the city's new school superintendent. Cheating with a pen and paper, she grimaced at the computer that had replaced her old electric typewriter and stacks of paper. Some things about modern journalism were just a bit much.

For instance, this neat, uncluttered, impeccable news-room. She sighed. Her first job had been on a weekly newspaper, in an office where visitors always seemed to giggle when they noticed the paper wadded and folded and sitting in lopsided stacks on the desk that probably had a top somewhere under all that clutter. A smile touched her mouth at the memory. Along with the clutter and the long hours and the variety of jobs—everything from writing to proofreading to pasting up to delivering the paper—had come a sense of belonging that made any sacrifice worthwhile. Then, too, there had been the aura of excitement that came with working for an editor who was already a legend—an awesome experience that time had never dulled.

Dana would never have left voluntarily. But her father's death and her mother's lingering illness that followed it had made it necessary. She moved to Miami, to a bigger job and a more specialized nursing home for her mother. The elderly woman was totally dependent on her doctors, totally oblivious to Dana and the world around her. And it took almost every spare penny Dana made to keep her there, although Dana would never have called it a sacrifice. Mrs. Meredith, in her day, had been a very special woman; it had taken the death of her husband to break that strong will.

"...Dana! Hey, girl, did that interview with the school super deafen you?" a loud voice called inches from her ear.

She jumped and looked up into the dancing blue eyes of the dark-haired girl at the next desk. "Sorry, Phyl, I wasn't listening. What?" she asked pleasantly, her eyebrows raised.

"I said, Jack wants you," she repeated, nodding toward the glass-enclosed office.

"Let's see," Dana murmured thoughtfully, one slender hand idly touching the taffy-colored hair in its severe bun, "I haven't used his phone in a week. I didn't paint green shamrocks on his hood on St. Patrick's Day. I didn't slip his name to the F.B.I. as a dangerous underground radical when those two agents were in the lobby last week. Okay," she said, getting up from the desk. "I've got nothing in this world to be afraid of. Except...well, I only *threatened* to stock his swimming pool with guppies, and that doesn't count.''

"Get out of here," Phyllis groaned. "You're giving me indigestion."

"Reporters don't get indigestion," Dana reminded her. "Reporters get ulcers."

"Not just reporters," Phyllis contradicted. "Honey, there are two kinds of people in this world—people who get ulcers, and people who give them. I've decided life is too short to be on the receiving end, so shake hands with a giver!''

"A giver?" the sports reporter asked, passing by. "Great! I'll take a couple of twenties, and a five—just until payday, of course.''

"I'm passing out ulcers, not money," Phyllis replied.

He stopped. "Oh. Well, in that case, I'll pass. Charlie gave me one of those last week, and I'm trying to trade it to Fred for his broken arm.''

Dana eased past him, with her back to

the wall. "I used to be sane," she told him. "Years ago, of course."

"Reporters are not sane," Phyllis broke in. "They become reporters because they can't get normal jobs…"

Dana ducked into Jack's office and closed the door. "You wanted to see me?" she asked the man behind the massive, cluttered desk.

He looked up at the slender young woman. Dana Meredith was pretty, but there was also something very innocent about her, something vulnerable. Maybe it was the soft brown eyes that seemed to dominate her face, or the taffy-colored hair she pulled into that tight bun on top of her head. Maybe it was the soft, pink mouth that always seemed to be smiling. He shrugged. He felt like a Roman throwing a Christian into the jaws of a lion.

And, in a sense, he was.

"There's no easy way to put it, honey," he said finally. "You're going to Atlanta on the eight a.m. flight to do a story on the Devereaux Textile Corporation."

She felt the blood drain out of her face,

the life drain out of her body. Too weak-kneed to even stand, she slumped into the nearest chair and caught her breath.

"At...Atlanta?" she whispered, her big eyes wide and frightened.

"Don't look at me like that," he groaned, dragging his husky form out of the chair. He turned to the window, running his hands restlessly through his thin hair. "Devereaux asked for you personally. He wants a major news piece on his new production methods, and he wants to give it to us—an exclusive, when it's the hottest copy south of the President. But there's a catch. He'll only give it to you."

She stared down at her cold, trembling hands. "Oh, my God," she whispered.

"It was three years ago," he reminded her.

She folded her arms across her chest, tight, close, as if they could protect her from what lay ahead. "I'd rather you fired me," she said unsteadily.

"That's what it's going to come down to. I'm sorry as hell, Dana, but Charlie wants it," he told her flatly. "That means your job, my job, both jobs go down the drain unless you pick up your nerve and go to Atlanta. Nobody says no to Charlie, remember?''

She closed her eyes. Charlie wants it. Three words that had given the newspaper a national reputation for excellence, for accuracy, for pure doggedness. And if she let them fire her, how would she live and support her mother until she could find another job in an already flooded field? The money was too good, and even the fury of Adrian Devereaux's black temper wasn't going to cost her this job. She owed him the last one, but not this one, and his vengeance wasn't costing her one more hour's peace!

She raised her face proudly. ''I'll go. I won't like it. I may never forgive you or Charlie for making me do it, but I'll go.''

''Look at it as a kind of rest period,'' Jack told her quietly. ''Just between us, you haven't been quite the same since you went to north Georgia to cover that flood. I know, it's been six months, but you never did let it out, Dana. I never once heard you mention it.''

The memory of it was worse than the one she carried of Adrian's dark, leonine face when he threw her out of his house. She flinched at the thought, pushing it immediately to the back of her mind.

''What was there to mention?'' she countered. ''It's over, like what I helped do to Adrian Devereaux. He trusted me, Jack. I applied for that job incognito, and lived in his house and worked for him weeks before he found out. He didn't know I was just there to do an exclusive about his wife's death and its effect on him. I tried to kill the story, but...'' She sighed. ''He was front page news, the editors had no choice.''

''I know the feeling,'' Jack said. ''Your story did help solve the case, eventually, too. It brought an eyewitness forward and led to the capture of the murderer.''

''It destroyed Adrian Devereaux,'' she said on a sigh. ''Financially at least. One word left out. When it should have read that his plants were not closing, the word 'not' was left out."

"Stock in his company plummeted overnight. He lost everything, I remember," Jack said, shaking his head. "Pity. But he's back on top again, now. Richer than ever, and he wants the world to know it."

"He wants me," she replied quietly. "He wants blood, and I've got to go and give it to him because Charlie wants the story."

"Three years is a long time," Jack reminded her. "He had you fired from that magazine, that should have been revenge enough for him."

She shook her head, staring blankly out the window. "You don't know him. He's a bulldozer. Relentless, unstoppable. I went to the lake with him and Lillian and some of his associates one weekend while I was working for him," she recalled. "I watched him angle for four hours trying to catch one particularly big bass. He did it. I never doubted that he would. He's waited three years for me, to pay me back for what I did to him. I expected it, too.''

''Dana, he wouldn't have waited that long...''

''He had to regain his finances first,'' she replied dully. ''Revenge can be expensive. You see, Jack, it isn't so much that I cost him his fortune as that I cost him his privacy. It was sacred to him.'' She laughed. ''You, *I*, we don't pay attention to our name in the paper, we're used to seeing our bylines. To the average person, it's something quite different. Adrian Devereaux worshiped his privacy; it was sacred to him. He trusted me, and I betrayed him. Yes, Jack, he'd wait three years to pay me back.''

He eyed her. ''Fate, Dana. You can plan your next step a thousand times, but it's never the one you expect.''

''Is that supposed to cheer me up?'' she asked.

''No,'' he said with a grin, ''it's supposed to remind you that it's easier to let life happen than it is to wear yourself out fighting it. You're still a kid.''

"Sure. Twenty-two and growing." She stood up. "I hope Charlie can afford a ticket for the flight."

"That, and more. All expenses, baby. And," he added quietly, "the boys and I will keep an eye on Mama for you while you're gone."

She fought a rush of tears and bit her lip at the intensity of emotion. Brash, boisterous, and sometimes outrageous, but were there people anywhere who cared as deeply as news people?

"Thanks," she whispered.

"Get out of here," he grumbled, going back to sit at his desk. "I've got an axe murder on Jackson Street and a Martian missionary calling every five minutes to send a reporter out to his spaceport to take pix of the invasion. Don't have me crying into the receiver when he calls back."

"I'll send you a postcard," she called over her shoulder.

"Of what," he retorted, "the sewing machines?"

"Where you off to now, love?" Phyllis

asked with a smile as she grabbed her purse and started toward the exit.

"The coliseum," she replied pleasantly and without breaking stride. "I'm going to feed the lions."

"Huh?" Phyllis asked.

But not a word floated back from the closing door.

Outside in the street, oblivious to the colorful jostle of passersby, the noise of traffic, the heat, she could feel her hands trembling with the cold of fear. Three years, but it might have been yesterday that Adrian Devereaux threw her out of the big brownstone house on its wooded preserve, leaving her to walk the mile and a half to the main gate with her dignity bruised and her eyes swelling with tears. It had been February, and snow was on the ground. Though it hadn't been deep—it was Atlanta, after all, not Chicago—it had been cold and wet and humiliating. Almost as humiliating as what came before. She could still see the cold anger in those dark, dark eyes when he found her out—when he accidentally found her news media card on the floor among the spilled contents of her purse. The tirade that had followed hadn't been at all pleasant. She thought she was prepared for anything, but she hadn't been, not for that horrible contempt, not for the sound of those adjectives hurled in his deep, measured voice. She hadn't been prepared because she hadn't thought she was emotionally involved. Not until he threw her out.

The years had only made the memories more potent. She could still think about him and feel the old excitement all over again. She could see that powerful, husky frame reclining in the big armchair in front of the fireplace, his face broad and strong and arrogant in the reflection of the orange flames as he dictated letters. She could hear the deep, clipped voice that held a dark authority, she could hear the quick, measured sound of footsteps in his den. She could feel the impact of his bold, slow eyes on her....

She glanced down the street in the direction from which the bus would eventually come. The traffic was bad, the fumes smothering like the spring heat. And all around her were other impatient travelers, just off from work and wanting to go home. Home. Atlanta was that to Dana.

She missed the city of her youth. Young and brassy, innovative architecture mixing with Confederate landmarks, a city of contrasts was the capital of Georgia. From the charred pyre of the Civil War South to the torch-bearer of Civil Rights, from Joel Chandler Harris to Margaret Mitchell, from the Cyclorama to Little Five Points, Atlanta was the sparkling jewel of the south. Elegance enough for an aristocrat, excitement enough for any adventurer, Atlanta had it all. Not to mention Ted Turner's Braves. Dana missed those home games and the sound of the big organ filling the stadium.

But best of all was Atlanta by night. A Christmas tree the year round. The colorful, shimmering lights of her nightclubs and restaurants and hotels and theaters sparkled all the way to the horizon like jewels against black velvet.

Dana sighed with the memory as the bus finally pulled up beside her small group, and she went inside with a silent prayer that she would find a handhold. She did.

She closed her eyes and lurched as the bus accelerated. Adrian. Adrian! It was definitely Tahiti time. When things got so bad that even the silver lining of the dark clouds was black, she threatened to chuck it all and go to Tahiti. Of course, she never did. It was an old joke, and everybody on the paper accepted it as such. But this time, if she'd had the money, she might just have gone.

Sure, she thought, I could chuck mother and the job to go live on a beach and eat bananas. I could scale Mt. Everest naked and barefoot, too. She sighed and opened her eyes. Her stop was coming up. As she got off, she wondered for the fiftieth time why Adrian had sent for her.

She was still wondering the next morning. Sitting aboard the Atlanta flight as it ate up the miles between Miami and the champagne city of Atlanta, she stared out at the clouds with eyes that didn't see. If only she could turn the clock back. If only she didn't have to get off the plane. If only elephants could fly...

It was raining when she left the plane at Hartsfield International Airport in Atlanta. A nice, slow drizzle, the kind that always made her want to curl up under a fuzzy blanket with a good book. But this particular day the rain seemed very much like tears....

She clutched her purse like a lifeline as she entered the terminal, nervously darting glances around the crowded, spacious interior with its sprinkling of booths. Jack had said that someone would meet her. He hadn't said who.

As she froze in her tracks, staring wildly ahead, she realized why he hadn't said who. Adrian Devereaux was coming straight toward her, and for one wild moment she thought she was going to faint.

Two

He looked older. There were lines in his face that hadn't been there the last time she saw him. The gray at his temples had spread into his thick, black hair. He was still husky and muscular, his build making him seem much taller than he actually was. He was, she thought dazedly, so good to look at. He always had been.

She gripped the purse as he stopped just in front of her. His dark, somber eyes took in her soft beige dress, her bare arms, the tight bun of her hair from which taffy-colored wisps hung rebelliously. He looked until her heart was shaking with its pounding, until her legs felt like spring saplings under her.

"Afraid, Meredith?" he asked gruffly, still using her surname for her first name, a holdover from her disguise as "Meredith Cane."

Her knuckles turned white on the purse. "No, sir, I'm not," she said in a husky voice, addressing him as she always had.

It brought back her first meeting with him, when she'd come sneaking in under his nose in the guise of his new private secretary. It had been a bold move, but with all the enthusiasm of a young reporter on her first major assignment, she'd carried the deception off with pure bravado.

"Can you take dictation?" he'd asked curtly, easing his husky frame into a chair that swallowed him but left space all around when she sat in it.

"Yes, sir," she'd returned just as curtly. "Backwards, forwards, and upside down, if you like."

"Upside down?" His dark, insolent eyes had traced a frankly sensuous path down her slender figure. "Won't your slip show, Meredith?"

She'd blushed. And he'd thrown back his head and roared like the lion he was. A lion, and she hadn't shown fear, and he'd respected her for that. Perhaps it had been just a bit more than respect, although he never went past skillful innuendos in their boss-secretary relationship before he found her out. Before he threw her out. Before he...

"You're thinner than I remember, Meredith," he said, his eyes narrow and glittering under the broad scowl. "Skinny might be an apt description."

"And you're heavier," she threw back, not pulling her punches. "And older," she added deliberately.

Something very like a flash of amusement touched the dark eyes. "I'm forty, in case you need reminding," he said. "I can give you eighteen years, little girl."

"Seventeen," she replied. "I'll be 23 this month."

He looked her over again, speculatively. "Aren't you going to ask why I told Charlie to send you?"

Her lower lip trembled despite her best effort at control. "I don't have to ask."

He searched her wan, tired face, hollow-eyed from lack of sleep. "No, you don't, do you?" he replied grimly.

She drew a deep breath. "Jack said I was to stay with you and Lillian," she said with as much dignity as she could muster. "I'd prefer a hotel."

"No doubt. But, you don't have a choice. You gave that up when you agreed to come, Persephone," he said, eyeing her coldly. "You always reminded me of her, Meredith, with your hair like honey and your face so damned innocent!"

She flushed to the edges of her hairline. "Why didn't you just hire a hit man and have me shot?" she asked shakily.

"Because I've waited a long time for this," he told her, "and I plan to enjoy every minute of it. Give me your claim check and I'll have Frank pick up your luggage."

She handed it to him automatically. He gestured, and a tall, thin man in a chauffeur's uniform joined him, took the baggage claim check and left.

"I didn't think you'd bother coming to fetch me yourself," she said coldly as he took her arm and walked her briskly toward the terminal entrance.

"The look on your face when you saw me was worth it," he said flatly.

She preceded him out the door to the gray Rolls parked at the curb, and let him put her inside. He went around the rear of the sleek automobile and slid in beside her.

She felt the car shake as Frank put the luggage in the boot, and again as he got in the driver's seat and the Rolls surged forward.

He shifted in the seat to face her, his jacket falling open over his broad chest under the white silk shirt he wore. "A reporter," he chided. "My God, it was the last thing I'd ever have guessed you were."

She stared down at the champagne-colored upholstery of the seat. "I'd like to tell you why I did it..."

"I already know."

She glanced at him quickly. How could he have known that the magazine promised her enough money to pay her mother's hospital expenses and doctor bills...

"I had you followed," he said darkly. "You were seen giving the money to a man, in a hotel restaurant! You damned little...!"

"Please, it wasn't what you...!"

"Shut up." He said it quietly, but in a tone that dared her to challenge him. "I didn't bring you back to think up bigger and better lies to explain yourself, Meredith."

She wanted to tell him that the man she was giving the money to was her father's attorney; that after her father's death, everything had to go to pay off debts. There wasn't enough to begin paying the specialists who were trying to repair what massive strokes had done to her mother. The money she earned from the magazine exclusive would have done that—although she refused the check when the story was run. She couldn't have borne to take it after what she'd done to Adrian. But he wouldn't listen. And even if he did, what difference did it make now whether he believed her or not?

"It was an insurance check from my father's death I was signing over to him," she wanted to say, "not blood money I got for selling the story that ruined you." But it was no use.

A large, darkly beautiful masculine hand with its ruby ring propped itself on the seat behind her. "Charlie mentioned you had responsibilities in Miami—someone you were supporting. Are you still keeping him up, Meredith?" he asked cruelly.

She met his eyes evenly. "My private life is none of your business, Mr. Devereaux. It never was."

"That's the damned truth. But mine was yours, wasn't it, little girl?" he growled. "I trusted you, dammit!"

She swallowed. "I know."

They were nearing the house, now. She watched the wooded, flowering grandeur of the long, paved driveway out the window as they neared the big brownstone house in its nest of oak, pine, and magnolia trees. There were flowers everywhere. Lillian's work, no doubt, because the thin little woman loved them so.

Lillian met her at the door. The wiry, silver-haired woman was just as Dana remembered her—brusque and efficient, but her brown eyes were as warm as a cozy fire in the hearth.

"Yes," Lillian said with a smile, eyeing the younger woman as they stood in the spacious foyer. "You're a bit older, but you haven't gained a pound. I'll have to fix that. Have you eaten?"

Dana managed a shaky smile, her ears listening for movement in the den where Adrian had gone as she stood in the light from the crystal chandelier that crowned the winding staircase.

"Yes, thank you," she told Lillian. "I had breakfast on the plane."

"You'll want coffee, though." The

smile faded as the older woman took stock of Dana's nervousness. "Don't worry now," she whispered stealthily. "It's not…"

"Lillian!" The voice was deep, curt, like rumbling thunder in the den, and so familiar that Dana wanted to cry. "Get some coffee and bring me a danish!"

"Yes, sir!" Lillian called back, and with a reassuring pat, she urged Dana toward the open door of the den. "He doesn't bite, remember," she said *sotto voce*.

"The hell he doesn't," Adrian answered. "Coffee, Lillian!"

"I'm going, I'm going, you don't have to yell…."

Dana stiffened her spine and walked numbly into the familiar cozy room with its Mediterranean decor, the huge oak desk, the leather sofa, and the big easy chair that bore the imprint of a big, husky body. He was standing with one arm resting on the mantle. There was a fire in the hearth to ease the chill of the room, and he was punching at it with a black poker.

"Sit down," he said without looking at her.

She perched herself on the very edge of the sofa, her purse crumpled and smudged under her restless fingers as she watched the way Adrian's dark hair gleamed in the firelight, a half-smile on the curve of his mouth. The ruby ring emphasized the darkness of that hair-sprinkled masculine hand that held the poker.

He put the poker away and turned to her. His fingers searched in his pocket for a cigarette. He dug out a slim gold lighter to put a flame to it, and inhaled deeply. His eyes narrowed on her wan face.

"Three years," he said quietly, "and I don't think you've been out of my mind for two days in all that time. Last month there was a feature story by you in that Florida magazine. It brought you back into my life with a vengeance, and I knew I had to see you again."

"What for?" she asked bitterly. "You had the picture."

"I could answer that question in a way that would turn you red from the roots of your hair all the way to your ankles," he said with a dark smile. "Can you still blush, I wonder, or have you lost the ability as well as your innocence?"

"I haven't lost either," she wanted to say, but Lillian came in with a tray of coffee and pastries, saving her a reply. By the time it was served and Lillian had gone again, the subject was forgotten.

"How long will I be here?" she asked dully.

His eyes studied her face intensely. "That's hard to say. Months, perhaps," he told her.

"I'd like a straight answer."

"You're getting one." He leaned back in his chair, the coffee cup in one hand, a cigarette smoking in the other. "I need a secretary."

"Not me."

"Don't bet on it." His eyes narrowed at her gasp of apprehension. "Charlie said Jack's been handling you with kid gloves ever since you covered some disaster last year, and he thinks you need a rest leave."

She blanched. "I don't...!"

"On the other hand," he continued calmly, "I lost my secretary about three weeks ago, and I can't replace him with just anyone. I need someone I can trust," he added deliberately. "And I doubt very seriously you'd make the mistake of betraying me a second time."

"I'm a reporter, not a..."

"You're not a reporter any more," he said coolly. "I called Charlie this morning."

"My job..." she croaked.

"...is being advertised in this morning's paper."

She jumped to her feet. "You can't do this!"

"The hell I can't. Sit down," he said, the old curt authority in his voice.

She collapsed down onto the soft leather. "Will you really take revenge this far?" she cried. "You don't understand, I can't stay here, away from Miami...!"

"You won't leave this house until I tell you to get out," he said coldly. "If you walk out that door, I'll break you. You won't ever get another job." He said it calmly, without ever raising his voice. And he meant it, every word.

Her eyes closed against the nightmare that was happening. "Please, I have to go home…!"

"This is home for the next six months." He finished the rest of his coffee. "You'll draw a salary, you'll be the private secretary you only pretended to be once before." His eyes narrowed, glittering, as he watched her reaction. "I want you for six months, Persephone. You caused me a hell of a lot of trouble, and I want recompense."

"I…I'll get a salary?" she managed weakly, her spirit completely gone as she realized just how completely she was at his mercy.

"More than you deserve," he replied, dropping heavily into the armchair across from her. He crossed his legs and watched her through narrowed eyes. "Enough, probably, to support your lover."

Her mouth trembled, and not for all the world would she have spoiled his vivid image of her. "Will I have…days off?"

"Occasionally."

"Can I go home...occasionally?"

"To see him? I don't think so."

Her eyes went misty. Mother...! "Oh, you can't...!"

"I can. I have." His dark eyes backed her down. "You owe me!"

She closed her eyes. Six months. To see him, be near him, be hated by him. Six months. Maybe she could get Jack and the boys to see about Mrs. Meredith. But six months...!

"I don't seem to have a choice," she whispered.

"In point of fact," he replied mildly, "you don't have any."

Her face jerked up rebelliously, one last flash of fury. "You damned Yankee!" she threw at him, referring pointedly to his Chicago origins, to the accent that lingered after half a lifetime spent in this city.

He actually grinned, his white teeth flashing in that dark, arrogant face. "You damned little rebel," he shot right back at her. "Welcome to hell, Persephone."

Her teeth ground together. "Thank you, Mr. Devil."

A glint of admiration touched his dark eyes before the mockery and anger came back into them.

"Still not afraid of me, Dana?" he asked softly, and it was the first time he'd ever used her real first name.

"No."

"That was why I hired you three years ago," he told her. "Because you'd fight me."

"You're the only person I ever have fought with," she returned with a glare. "I get along with most people. It isn't in my nature to…"

"You don't know what your nature is yet," he said. "We're going to work on that. I think your education has some gaps that need filling in."

"School's out," she said shortly.

"Just beginning," he corrected. "It's time we got around to discussing the more mundane aspects of your new job."

Somehow, she got through that hour, listening to his deep, measured voice, only half hearing the instructions. It was three years ago, and she was in awe of him again. Involuntarily, her eyes traced every line of his face while he spoke, loving him all over again. How had she lived those years without seeing him, hearing him? How had she managed to survive, when just to be in the same room with him was all that she needed of paradise?

In between keeping those soulful glances hidden from him, she managed to digest the better part of her new duties. It was like old times. To stand between him and the outside world. To protect his privacy from intrusion. To make his appointments and reservations and see that he kept them, to take dictation any time of the night or day, to keep his social calendar and be his memory. And do it without any lip. And when he added that, she glared at him, and he grinned for the second time since her return.

He left her with three letters to type and a backlog of appointments to confirm or cancel, and she didn't move from the room until it was time to clean up for the evening meal.

She took a quick shower and dressed in a beige jersey dress that clung to her "skinny" figure, and put her hair up in its familiar bun. In between wondering how she was going to look after her mother from this distance, and how harsh Devereaux's revenge was going to be, she felt the old, sweet fires beginning to kindle inside her. The sudden shock of seeing him gave her fluttery sensations in the pit of her stomach, and made her face glow with the bright flame of pleasure. She thrilled to the sound of his voice, deep and masculine and quiet. Her eyes closed as she sank into the armchair by her fireplace. Why did this house feel so much like home? It had, from the first time she saw it, so many years ago, big and imposing and immovable—just like its master. With a sigh, she got up and glanced at her pale face in the mirror, dominated by wide, soft brown eyes, and shook her head. She put a touch of pale pink lipstick on her mouth and went downstairs.

She felt his dark eyes on her while she tried to eat the delicious meal Lillian had prepared—which tasted vaguely like cardboard under the circumstances.

"Is your steak overdone, Meredith?" he asked across the short distance that separated them, sitting there like some dark monarch in his faultlessly tailored gold-patterned silk shirt and brown close-fitting slacks. The shirt was open just enough over his broad chest to be sensual, letting the dark mat of hair that covered the unyielding muscles peek out.

"My steak is just fine, thank you," she replied smoothly. "I'm...not very hungry."

He lifted his coffee up to his chiseled, wide mouth.

"Aren't you? I wonder why?" His lips curved as he studied her, his eyes narrow and glittering so that it was impossible to tell their color.

She glanced at him accusingly. "Are you enjoying yourself, Mr. Devereaux?" she asked quietly. "This must be something like sticking a sharp pin into a butterfly to see how much pain it can take.''

His dark, beautiful hand curved around his glass and he studied the burgundy shimmer of the wine under the light from the chandelier. "Pain can create a kind of pleasure, Meredith,'' he said, and his eyes met her levelly. "It can even enhance the pleasure. You can't make wine without crushing the grape.''

"You must know a lot about crushing,'' she murmured.

"I do,'' he said matter-of-factly, leaning back in his chair with one arm curved over its back, straining the silk shirt across the powerful, broad muscles of his chest.

She dragged her eyes away from him, back down to her plate. "What…what about the new production method I was supposed to do a story on?'' she asked. "Was that part of the fiction, too?''

"No. You'll get a look at that before you leave here. And a story, Meredith,'' he said contemptuously. "My God, do you bleed ink? Is everything you do just part of the damned job?''

She flinched at the violence in his tone. "They say that a good reporter can pull copy out of the worst disaster," she said in a subdued tone. Her eyes closed with the memory of the flood. "God help us, we can, too," she added in a murmur.

He set the wine glass down with a thud and stood up. "As much as I'd love to continue this fascinating conversation," he said, "I've got a date. Don't choke on your wine, Persephone."

She watched him go, slinging his jacket over one arm, his step even, ruthless. He was in superb physical condition, an athlete who thrived on sports, and there wasn't a spare ounce of flesh on that broad, powerful body. He walked with a leonine grace, and she felt a stab of jealousy as she heard him go out the door. A date. A woman. She stared with blank eyes at the steak on her plate. And why not, he wasn't over the hill. He was still a virile, utterly masculine man. Naturally there would be women. There were women when she worked for him. It had hurt then, and it hurt now. She didn't have the sophistication, or the charm to catch a man like Adrian Devereaux, and she knew it. That hurt most of all. With a tiny shudder, she pushed the plate aside and left the table.

"The Mister gone already?" Lillian asked as Dana started up the stairs to her room.

She managed a weary smile for the older woman. "In a blaze of glory," she laughed.

"As usual. It's that Fayre Braunns again, I'll bet," Lillian said darkly. "None of my business, of course, but that blonde dragon gives me goose bumps."

"She's his…girlfriend?" Dana asked.

"His mistress," Lillian corrected, with a smile at the shock on the other woman's face. "He's all man, honey. You can't expect him to be a saint, can you?"

She smiled. "He never was, I imagine. What's Fayre like?"

"Blonde, beautiful, and expensive, just like the ones before her. She's the latest in a string." Her narrow eyes studied the young, blond sapling on the stairs. "You

make him keep his distance, young lady,"
she said suddenly. "Don't let him hurt
you. He can, you know. You're just a
baby."

Dana blushed. "You must know why he
had me sent here," she murmured, "and
how much contempt..."

"I know what he says," Lillian corrected. "The Mister's deep, and nobody
can read him, not even me and I've been
here eighteen years. But I think he sent for
you for more than just a chance to get
even. Be careful."

"You don't need to tell me that he's
dangerous," Dana said quietly, turning toward the stairs. "He cost me my job and
my peace of mind, and now he's going to
keep me in bondage for six months. I'll
bet in his spare time he teaches ants how
to torture their aphids."

Lillian tried to stifle a giggle and failed.
"Just the same," she said, sobering, "it's
strange to me that he waited this long for
vengeance."

"Don't lose any sleep over it. I can take
care of myself. I've been doing that for a

long time." She gave Lillian a smile and started up the steps. "Goodnight."

"Goodnight, honey. Sleep well."

Dana almost laughed at that. It had been months since she'd slept well. Months...

She was in the middle of a business letter the next morning when the phone rang. She answered it absently, her mind on the letter and a clipped voice replied.

"Let me speak to Adrian," it said shortly.

"He isn't here right now," she replied in a businesslike tone. "May I take your number and have him return the call?"

"I'm just passing through," the voice said after a slight hesitation. "My name's Dick Black—you may have heard him mention me, we were in Vietnam together. Gosh, I hate to leave town without saying hello, we shared a hooch and dodged bullets together!"

Dana hesitated. If she let his old buddy leave town without trying to get in touch with her boss, she knew she was going to catch it from both sides.

"Here," she said abruptly, "let me give you his number at the office, and you can contact him there."

"Hey, thanks, you're a pal!" came the cheerful reply.

It was only after she hung up that she remembered the old warning he hadn't bothered to reemphasize. Never, but never, give out his private number at work to anyone. But, she reminded herself, Dick Black wasn't anybody, surely. An old war buddy did have some privileges, didn't he? She went back to the letter she was typing and forgot about it.

It had been a busy day, and she was just finishing up when the front door opened with a violent snap. She tensed at the heavy, angry footsteps in the hall and turned just in time to meet a pair of slitted, glittering eyes in a face like thunder.

Adrian Devereaux slammed his attache case down flat on his big oak desk. With one hand deep in his pocket, he stood studying her grimly.

"Do you enjoy getting under my skin, Meredith?" he asked in a voice gone soft, almost tender in his fury. "Do you lay awake nights thinking up ways to annoy me?"

She swallowed nervously, clutching her skirt in her fingers. "What have I done?" she asked, uneasily.

"What the hell do you think?" he growled, slamming his hand down palm first on the surface of the desk. "Are you working with the wire services on the side, or was that newsman some old friend you owed a favor to?"

"I...you know I'm not working for anybody except you," she returned. "What newsman?"

"Good old Dick Black," he shot at her.

She covered her mouth. "Oh, no," she breathed.

"Oh, yes, and you needn't pretend you didn't know! Damn you, Meredith, I could shake you until your teeth break!" he said hotly, glaring at her. "If I told you once, I told you a half-dozen times to never, *never* give out my office number!"

"I know," she whispered, "but he said..."

"To hell with what he said!" He glared at her across the desk, his face stony, his eyes like slits of fire. She felt her knees give way under the cut of his gaze.

"I'm sorry," she whispered, tears welling involuntarily in her eyes. The strain was getting to her—his hatred, worrying about her mother, the nightmares...

He froze, as if the reply wasn't the one he'd been expecting. "What?"

She turned away, fighting for composure, shaking her head as if to dismiss her reply.

"Meredith?" His voice was deeper than usual, quiet.

She drew herself together and let her eyes drift up to his collar, but no further. "I'm sorry. It won't happen again."

There was a pause while he lit a cigarette. Her eyes went to his heavily-lined face as he perched himself on the edge of the desk, and shot a glance at her.

"I want to give a party this weekend," he said, changing the subject abruptly. "At the cabin, for about twelve couples. Arrange it. Supper and snacks and booze."

"Yes, sir. Do you want the caterer you used last..."

"Yes. And don't forget the music."

"A live band?"

He glared at her. "Of course, Meredith, a live one."

She flinched inwardly at the sarcasm and made herself a note on her steno pad, no outward sign of her emotional turmoil showing. That seemed to light a fire under his temper.

"I'll give you a list of the guests later," he said in a voice that had suddenly chilled. "You're to call each one, individually, and confirm their attendance."

"Yes, sir."

"Cool, aren't you?" he asked harshly. "Does anything touch you? Do you feel?"

"I feel what I have to," she replied calmly, determined not to let him see her lose that hard won composure. She stood up, pale and drawn, but outwardly quite unruffled. "Is that all, sir?"

"Yes, damn you, that's all," he said in a harsh whisper.

She walked out with her head high, the

tiny triumph bringing a smile to her lips as she went.

She hid in the kitchen with Lillian while waiting for him to calm down.

"Bad, huh?" Lillian asked with a conspiratorial whisper and with a smile.

Dana nodded. "Oh, he can be such a…"

"Don't say it, I get the general idea. Sit down, honey, and talk to me while I get dinner."

Dana dropped onto one of the chairs and sat with her chin in her hands, dejected and miserable. "He's a beast." She got up and went to the cupboard, taking out a cup.

"There's a reason," Lillian said quietly, eyeing Dana while she rolled a piecrust, her brown hands flecked with flour and dough. "He's so alone."

"We all are," Dana said absently, her eyes blank on the shimmering black coffee as she poured herself a cup of the steaming brew and sat back down. "Every one of us."

"Not like he is." Lillian picked up the pie tin and a sharp knife, and trimmed the excess pastry away in a neat motion. "And I don't mean just since the Missus died. She hated him. Hated his job, hated his hobbies, hated his civic work…she was jealous of him. If you'd worked here while she was still alive, she'd have made life hell for you. She drove him wild with her jealousy. You know," she said solemnly, setting down the pie crust to study Dana, "she used to call restaurants where he'd be entertaining clients, to see who he was with. She was always checking up on him."

Dana nodded. "I remember hearing you talk about it, years ago. He…he was a very attractive man, I don't suppose she could help being jealous if she loved him."

"That's the whole point, she didn't," Lillian said gruffly. "She didn't care if he died, but she was scared he'd find some other woman and kick her out. She liked the money, the clothes, the fancy cars. She liked her life, and didn't have any notion of changing it."

"But she had lovers…"

"Only the one who killed her," Lillian

recalled. "He was special, but when the Mister told her to give him up, she didn't give it a second thought. They said that was why her lover killed her, because she was breaking it off. She'd given him God knows how many expensive things, including a car...the trial cut the Mister apart," she said, shaking her head. "It ripped his pride to shreds, but I never heard him say a word about it. Not one word. He buried it inside."

Something else for him to blame me for, Dana thought miserably. To lose his fortune and his pride at the same time would have been a blow few men could have borne. But Adrian Devereaux was a breed apart, and nothing could bring him to his knees.

"He loved her?" she murmured absently.

"Honey, you can't live with someone for thirteen years and not feel anything when they die," Lillian said with a patient smile. "I think he had to feel something for her. She was a very beautiful woman, and she could be charming. But she sure didn't care about him. Wouldn't even give him children—she was afraid they'd ruin her figure.''

''Maybe he didn't want them,'' she murmured.

Dana felt those wise eyes on her. ''He wanted them. There's a child-hunger in that man. He wants an heir. But,'' she added coolly, ''he needn't think this new girl's going to give him one! She likes her girlish figure, too, for all that her girlhood years are behind her,'' she mumbled cattily.

''Is she his age?''

''Just about.'' Lillian smiled. ''You're a baby compared to both of them. You steer clear of the dragon, honey, she'll burn you to a cinder.''

''I can't. He's getting me up a list of people to invite to a party on the lake this weekend. I'll just bet her name's at the top of the list.''

''God love you, child,'' Lillian sighed. She poured the apple mixture into her pie shell and laid the second crust on top, pinching the edges together in a pretty fluted pattern. Just as Dana's mother used to do, years ago, before...

"He hates me, you know," she told Lillian, tracing the pattern on the tablecloth with one long, slender finger.

"Why?" Lillian asked quietly. "If you hadn't written that story, somebody else would have. And if something's meant to happen, young one, it will."

"You're a fatalist."

"You betcha. The Mister hates what happened, but I don't think he'd carry a grudge that far that long," she said firmly, wiping her hands. She opened the oven door and shot the pie in, closing it gently. "He'll get over it."

"I should live so long," Dana murmured, pushing her taffy-colored hair back into her bun. "He's got me for six months, and I promise I'll pay for sins I haven't even thought of committing before he's through with me. He can be so ruthless, Lillian."

"And so blind."

Dana met the older woman's sharp eyes. "Blind?" she echoed.

Lillian returned her attention to the remains of the pie crust and began to clean it up. "Tell me what you've been doing for the past three years."

"If I can have another cup of coffee, I'll give you all the inside gossip about that society murder in Miami earlier this month."

"The one where the main suspect was found dead with his mistress?" Lillian asked, wide-eyed.

"The very same."

"Here," she said, handing Dana the coffee pot. "And I'll throw in a homemade sweet roll. Start talking."

Three

She got through the week, but her nerves were almost in shreds by the end of it. Confirming those miserable invitations had been an inhuman test of her temper. The men liked her husky voice and wanted to flirt. The women wanted to know why "Adrian" wasn't extending personal invitations, and who was Dana? But the dragon was the worst of all. The very worst.

"Hello," the reply came when Dana

reached Fayre Braunn's residence, in a voice like silk and honey.

"Miss Braunns, I'm calling for Adrian Devereaux," Dana said in the pat speech she'd rehearsed. "He'd like you to join him at a party on the lake Saturday night about seven. He'll pick you up at your apartment at six."

"Who are you?" Fayre asked haughtily, all the silk and honey turning bitter.

"I'm Dana Meredith, Mr. Devereaux's private secretary."

"Well, well, he hasn't mentioned *you*. How long have you worked for him?"

"A week, Miss Braunns. Will you attend the party?"

"Oh, good heavens, of course I will! How old are you, Miss Meredith?" the voice purred.

"Eighty-six. And a half," she added tartly. "I'll tell Mr. Devereaux you'll be ready. Goodbye." She hung up on the gasp at the other end of the line. Her chest rose in an agitated sigh. She knew she'd catch hell for that piece of effrontery, but she didn't regret it. Not one little bit.

She didn't regret it until she heard him come into the den, and turned and saw the familiar black anger written all over his heavily lined face.

"You, madam," he said levelly, "are pushing your luck over a cliff. I've just spent the past hour calming a very irritated tigress who seems to have the idea that I'm harboring a kept woman!"

"If you mean the dra...I mean, Miss Braunns," she corrected quickly, "she was more interested in interrogating me than she was in accepting..."

"I don't give a damn. If she wants to know the color of your pajamas, Meredith, you tell her!" His eyes narrowed, glittering down as he stood over her at the desk. "By God, you're an employee here, not the mistress of the house dispensing invitations!"

She felt every muscle in her body contract at the icy attack, and it took every bit of will power she possessed to keep her composure. "Excuse me, I didn't realize that the job involved selling my pride as well."

"It involves whatever I say it involves. You were rude, Miss Priss, and deliberately." His jaw set. "Never again, do you understand me? Or I'll set you down in a way you'll grow old trying to forget!"

She raised her face, a calm expression pasted to it. "Yes, sir. It won't happen again, sir. I'm very sorry sir."

His hands clenched into huge fists on the surface of the desk, the knuckles going white. He drew a heavy, harsh breath and turned away, going to stand at the window with his hands jammed into his pants pockets.

"I've never known a woman who could get under my skin the way you do," he growled. "God, you make me want to do something violent...!"

"If I were a man, you'd hit me, wouldn't you?" she asked matter-of-factly. "Then, I'm very glad I'm not a man, Mr. Devereaux, because I don't imagine you pull your punches."

He glanced at her hotly. "I don't. Any more than you pull yours." He studied her pale face. "Just how deep does that veneer of composure go, Meredith?'' His lips narrowed. ''One day, I'm going to strip you out of it and see what's underneath.''

She avoided his eyes and rose from the desk. ''I'm through for the day. Do you mind if I help Lillian in the kitchen, sir?''

He hesitated. ''Hell, go ahead.'' He lit a cigarette. ''Don't tell me cooking's among your many talents?''

She paused with her hand on the doorknob. ''I'm very good with hemlock and toadstools,'' she said quietly.

''No doubt.'' He didn't say another word as she left.

Supper was frigid. Utterly frigid. She'd tried to take refuge in the kitchen with Lillian, but he wouldn't hear of that. With a thread of pure anger in his deep voice, he'd practically ordered her to his table. And watched her relentlessly while she picked at her food.

''If you don't eat,'' he said finally, leaning back in the chair to watch her through narrowed eyes, ''I'll feed you myself.''

Her head jerked up and her lips started to form words.

"Oh, hell, yes, I will," he said, anticipating her protest. "You've lost at least three pounds since you've been here. I want a healthy secretary, Meredith, not a sickly scarecrow, do you understand me? Now, eat!"

She lifted the food to her lips with numb fingers, barely tasting the perfectly seasoned rice, the deliciously tender veal. Not, "I'm concerned about you, take care of yourself"—but, "I need your services, stay well." Damn him, he didn't have an ounce of kindness in his whole body, she thought, hurting from the onslaught. She finished her dinner, drank her coffee, and finally escaped to the kitchen where she spent the rest of the evening with Lillian.

She had started up the stairs to bed when, on an impulse she went out the door instead and into the garden.

It was a warm, spring night, and the scent of white roses was everywhere. In the pale moonlight, they seemed to glow, a delicate fantasy of beauty spreading over the gentle slope of the lawn in manicured perfection. She paused on the brick walkway and touched one of them, pressing it to her cheek as she inhaled the sweet fragrance.

"Looking for unicorns, Meredith?"

She jumped, startled by the deep, curt voice, and pricked her finger on a thorn as she turned to see the master of the house standing a few feet behind her. His jacket and tie were gone and his shirt was open halfway down that massive chest, revealing bronzed skin and a mat of black, curling hair. His dark slacks hugged his narrow hips and his powerful legs as he stood, one hand in his pocket and the other holding a cigarette. His whole posture was threatening.

"I...I don't believe in unicorns anymore, Mr. Devereaux," she said in a thin voice, touching the pricked finger to her lips, amazed that he'd remembered that long-ago conversation...

"You used to," he said quietly. "We stood here in the garden and talked about myths, and I told you I was past the age of believing in them. And you said that you did."

"That was a long time ago."

"Three years?" He drew the cigarette to his broad, chiseled mouth. "Long enough. Has reporting made you cynical, little girl? Has it made you bloodless, painless, invulnerable?"

She shuddered, although the night was warm, hearing that rescue worker's voice in her mind as she'd heard it for six months, "What the hell are you people, vultures?! My God, you're making a carnival out of it…!"

"NO!" The word broke from her, and she clasped her hands around her shaking body and turned away from him, with a knife-like pain in her heart. She took a deep breath.

"What's the matter, Meredith?" He moved closer. "Did I hit a nerve?"

She closed her eyes. "I…finished the invitation calls," she said, businesslike and calm again. "Do you have anything in particular for me to get out tomorrow, sir?"

He drew a sharp breath, as if he didn't like the change of subject, and turned away. He started rattling off chores, and her mind wandered briefly away to the sound of angry voices and weeping and yelled commands...

"...need that letter out first thing in the morning," he was saying as she forced her mind back to the present. "And cancel that Rotary Club speech, I don't have time. Think you've got all that, Meredith?" he asked gruffly.

She nodded. "Yes, sir. What about Mr. Samson? He was supposed to meet you for a drink after the Rotary meeting."

"Efficient, aren't you?" he growled, his dark eyes narrow and angry in the soft white moonlight.

"You pay me to be efficient, Mr. Devereaux," she said primly. "What about Mr. Samson?"

"Tell him I'll meet him for lunch Friday at the country club."

"You can't," she reminded him. "You have to be in Chicago Friday to discuss the Shore contract."

"Then Monday."

"Yes, sir." She turned away.

"Meredith?"

"Yes, sir?"

There was a hesitation, about the space of a heartbeat. "Walk with me."

Confused, she turned and fell into step beside him, his behavior making her mind spin. From anger to companionship in seconds, his lightning mood changes stunned her. He wasn't a tall man, she thought, noticing that he was barely half a head taller than she was in her three-inch heels. But he was so big, so broad and leonine, that he seemed to tower over people. Warmth and power radiated from him, a dark, strong warmth that made her want to feel the strength in his arms... She flicked her eyes toward the house, trying to ignore the buried longings that his company was resurrecting.

He took a long draw from his cigarette. "Why reporting?" he asked conversationally. "Why not fashion or advertising?"

She watched the shimmer of moonlight on the dewy grass. "Because I could write. I never wanted to do anything else. At first," she recalled, smiling, "I wanted to be a novelist. But I found out that a lot of people wanted to be novelists, people with more talent than I'd ever have. So I settled for truth instead of fiction.''

''Truth?'' he asked quietly.

She withdrew, like a child that had stretched its hand toward a warm, welcoming flame, only to have it burned. ''I'm sorry.''

He laughed mirthlessly. ''You cost me a fortune. And you're sorry.''

She closed her eyes against the hurt. ''I tried to tell you that I didn't leave the word out. It was there, on my copy, when the magazine came out...!''

''Was it?'' he growled.

''Would you like to hit me?'' she asked, stopping in her tracks to turn her pale haunted face up to his. ''If it would make you feel better, then go ahead! I've been hurt so much already, I won't even feel it!''

He stopped too, his eyes sliding over her face, her throat. ''What I'd like to do to you doesn't bear telling,'' he said with a soft fury in his voice. ''I haven't forgotten that sleazy character I saw you with, that bald-headed fat man you took for a lover! Damn you…!''

"I'd like to go in now, please," she said, her voice a husky shadow of sound in the darkness. "I'm very tired."

"What have you done to make you so tired, Meredith?" he demanded, slinging the finished cigarette into the darkness. "What have you done besides answer the phone and type letters?"

"Been slowly crucified by you!" she almost screamed, desperation in her eyes, her voice, her posture.

He moved closer, until he was within easy touching distance, until she could feel the heat of his big, vibrant body, until his dark face filled the world. One hand came out of his pocket, one dark, beautiful hand with square-tipped, broad fingers that caught her soft throat like a fleshy vise and caused her pulse to do cartwheels.

"What did you expect when I sent for you?" he asked slowly, his fingers absently caressing the silken flesh of her throat. "That I wanted you here because you were haunting my dreams, because my life was empty and cold without you in it? Did you think I sent for you out of love, Meredith?!''

She felt tremors running the length of her slender body. His nearness was as much the cause of it as fear. She could feel his warm breath on her forehead, smell the sharp, musky scent of his cologne, feel the hardness of him as if he were already holding her. She wanted to move closer, to feel him against the length of her softness, to touch that hard, dark chest with its curling mat of hair...

''I...I don't know,'' she stammered. I...I...''

''You're stammering, little girl,'' he murmured, a dangerous softness in his deep voice as his other hand went down to her waist, drawing her against his big body with a lazy tenderness that made her tremble. Her cold hands pressed patterns into the warmth of his cotton shirt over that warm, unyielding chest.

''Please don't,'' she whispered.

''Why not?'' he asked.

"Because it won't mean anything," she replied easily. The feel of that powerful driving masculinity so close against her was like a narcotic.

His thumb moved softly, gently against the softness of her mouth, his fingers coaxing her cheek against his warm shoulder so that he could look down into her eyes.

"Little girl," he whispered deeply. "You used to sit and watch me, like some little golden kitten, while I dictated letters late at night by the fireplace. I can still see that look in your eyes—soft and curious and just a little hungry. God, you were vulnerable then! Mine for the asking, if I'd realized it...a sweet little innocent, ripe for the picking, and I was too damned blind to notice that you wanted me to pick you."

"I didn't!" she whispered frantically, pushing at his solid chest.

"You did, and we both know it," he growled, his eyes narrow and flashing dark fire as his hand at her back tightened. "I never touched you," he whispered. "Never, not one time, but I wanted to...!"

His head bent, his eyes still holding

hers, his big arm tightening like steel, holding her, hurting her.

"Oh, please, Adrian, don't do this…" she pleaded gently.

He stopped. Froze. His eyes searched her face as if he'd never seen it before. "Say my name again," he said.

"Adrian…"

His fingers traced the soft, fluid line of her flushed cheek as he watched her in a static burning silence. "Doe eyes," he murmured. "As lovely as a fawn. Soft and sweet and vulnerable. You're trembling, little one, I can feel it. Do I make you hungry, Meredith? Do you want to taste me?" he whispered, his hard, chiseled mouth hovering half a breath over hers as she breathed in the musky, male scent of him, her heart shaking her with its pounding.

"Devil…" she sobbed as his hard mouth teased hers, tormented it with a whisper-light pressure that was no pressure, setting fires in her blood' "devil…straight out of hell!"

"Do I make you burn, Persephone?" he

murmured against her parted, pleading lips. "Do I make you hungry?"

"Y...yes! Adrian...!" she choked.

His teeth nipped lightly at her delicate upper lip, in a smoky, sensuous caress. Both his hands were buried in her thick, silky hair now, holding her face up to his.

"What is it, honey?" he whispered, his mouth touching her closed eyelids, her cheeks, the corner of her lips with slow, brief kisses.

"Oh...please..." she breathed, tears misting her eyes at the hunger he was kindling, a hunger like nothing she'd ever experienced. Her nails dug into him through the soft fabric of his shirt, though she was barely aware of the contact.

He laughed softly, deeply, "Do I make you that hungry, little cat?" he whispered. "Do you want to claw me?"

"D...damn you!" she wept.

His lips burned her in a brief, biting kiss. "Beg me for it," he murmured gruffly.

"I hate you!" she cried, her voice breaking, tears streaming down her cheeks as she looked up into his eyes with the agony of the damned in her wide, misty dark eyes.

His hands tightened around her head, his gaze dark and quiet and shadowy. "Where's all that majestic composure now, young Meredith?" he asked harshly. "By God, I told you I'd strip that veneer of sophistication away before I was through. Under it, you're every inch a woman, aren't you?"

Tears rolled uncontrollably down her cheeks and she closed her eyes against the humiliation. His hands dropped to her shoulders and he gripped them painfully and shook her. "Stop it," he said in glacial tones. "My God, what are you crying about?"

She shuddered with the memory of her own voice pleading... "Will you let me go?" she whispered icily.

"That isn't what you wanted a minute ago," he reminded her cruelly as he released her and turned away to light a cigarette.

She wrapped her arms around her shivering body and took a deep, shuddering breath. The tears were like tiny ice trails down her cheeks where the breeze hit them.

"Hail the suffering heroine," he taunted. "Why pretend, Persephone? These virginal displays don't affect me one way or the other, we both know that illusion of innocence doesn't go any deeper than your integrity."

"You don't know anything about me, Mr. Devereaux," she said with what dignity she could muster. "Not anything at all."

"I know you're easily aroused," he said.

"That isn't hard for any man who's experienced, is it?" she asked bitterly. "And you obviously are."

"Could he make you burn that easily?" he asked in a voice that cut like a whip.

"He?" she echoed.

"Your lover! The man you're supporting!" he threw at her.

"I'm not supporting any man, and I've never had a lover in my life!" she all but screamed at him. "Did you take lessons in cruelty, Mr. Devereaux, or does it come naturally to you? Why don't you just cut me into little pieces and be done with it!"

He took a draw from the cigarette he'd just lit and watched her narrowly. "When you're through having hysterics, I've got another letter to dictate."

Hysterics! She raised a trembling hand to her face, brushing away the tears. Her heart felt like a dead weight in her chest. She wanted to lie down someplace quiet and just die.

He was behind her suddenly, his big hand outstretched with a soft white handkerchief. "Dry your eyes, little girl," he said, and his voice was almost kind.

She took it wordlessly and dabbed at her eyes, blowing her nose. She clutched it in her hand like a lifeline.

"I'll get my pad," she said, raising her face proudly, her red-rimmed eyes meeting his levelly.

He watched her walk into the house, her spine as straight as a slide rule, her carriage faultless. With her back to him, she didn't see the look that was carved on his dark face.

Four

The drive up to Devereaux's cabin on Lake Lanier took barely an hour, even in the weekend traffic, but to Dana and Lillian it seemed much longer.

"I hate riding," Lillian confided as Frank helped them unload their preparations from the sleek Lincoln. "I like being there and being back, but I hate the in-between."

Dana only laughed, her eyes on the red-wood cabin, so spacious and majestic in its woodsy setting on the lakefront. It boasted huge picture windows and sliding glass doors and a fireplace that must have been heaven to sit by in winter.

It was the perfect setting for a party, with the wide pier on the lake and the boat dock next to it, and the beautiful clean silence of bark and grass and brown earth.

Dana paused on the wide front porch overlooking the lake and let the cool wind tear at her loosened hair. She'd stood here with him once, at night, and listened to the sound of dogs baying in the distance. And listened to his deep voice as he told her about the old days when he hunted the Georgia mountains with his father in the fall, while he was growing up in Chicago.

"Beautiful, isn't it?" Lillian sighed, pausing beside her. "Peace and quiet and birds and wind rustling the trees. This place keeps the Mister sane, I'll tell you. It's his refuge."

"Why does he want to ruin it with a houseful of drunk people?" Dana wanted to know.

"Still a teetotaler, are you?" Lillian

teased. "Baby, you just can't understand why people drink, can you?"

Remembering last night, Dana felt a shudder run through her. "Oh, I've got a good idea. Lillian, do you think that band's reliable?"

"Sure they are. Don't worry, now, everything's going to be just fine. Trust me. Nothing's going to go wrong."

Sure, Dana thought to herself when the band leader called fifteen minutes before he was due to arrive with his group and told her there'd been a car wreck. Fortunately, no one was hurt badly, but they wouldn't be able to perform.

That was just the tip of the iceberg. She'd forgotten to get a bag of ice, and there was none in the refrigerator. The ham she'd wrapped so lovingly flew out of her hands as she tripped on the steps and went rolling down into the lake.

She sat down on the front stoop, her face in her hands, with ten minutes to get everything ready before Devereaux and his party arrived.

"Dana, what are you doing?" Lillian called, her apron waving in the wind.

"I'm having a nervous breakdown?!" she replied.

"Where's the ham?"

Dana pointed toward the shore, where the lake was lapping gently around the lovely huge party ham.

"And the band?"

"They were in a wreck and they can't come. They're very sorry," she added.

"My God!"

"It's all right," Dana told her reassuringly. "He'll only drown me once, you know."

"What will we do?" Lillian was muttering to herself, as if she could hear the funeral dirge being played slowly in the distance.

Dana got up. "I'll fix it. Reporters," she told the older woman, "are resourceful. Or they get barbecued by city editors."

She got on the phone and called an old friend at the local daily paper. From her, she got the name of a good local band, which could be had, fortunately, on the spur of the moment, and the address of a good local deli. She sent Frank for cold cuts, called the band and in five minutes had everything wrapped up.

"Magic," Lillian murmured, shaking her head in awe.

"Unicorns," Dana laughed. "I believe in them, you know."

She stayed in the kitchen with Lillian when the guests began to arrive, every one of them late, and the band was already winding up its first number by the time Adrian Devereaux arrived—with the dragon.

Fayre Braunns was the perfect foil for Adrian's satanic darkness. She was blond, petite, with eyes so big and green that they seemed to dominate her sharp face. She was wearing a white lace pantsuit that clung like skin to her slender figure, contrasting violently with the dark brown silk of Adrian's open shirt and white slacks. They made the perfect couple, Dana had to admit, feeling an emptiness in the region of her heart as she watched the blonde cling to him.

She hadn't dressed for the occasion, wearing faded denims and a blue and white checked knit top, but the sweep of her blond hair gave the old clothes an elegance she wasn't aware of.

She was finishing another tray of bacon-rolled dates for canapes when she heard the door open behind her.

"I'll have this batch ready in a jiffy, Lillian," she said cheerfully, arranging parsley around the edges of the tray.

"Hiding, Meredith?"

She tensed at the sound of that deep voice, her muscles contracting when she felt him move closer, felt the warm vibrancy of his powerful body just behind her, almost touching.

It was the first contact she'd had with him since the argument, and she didn't want it at all.

"Lillian and I thought it would be better if we shared the kitchen chores while we were here," she murmured.

"Did you?" His big hands slid onto her waist, drawing her gently, slowly back against him so that she could feel the hard muscle of his thighs, his flat stomach, his chest. His breath was warm beside her ear.

"What are you making?" he asked.

"They...they're date and bacon rolls," she whispered.

"What do they taste like?"

Impulsively, she picked up one of the tasty morsels and, turning slightly, held it to his chiseled mouth. He took it, his lips brushing her fingers as he savored it.

"Not bad," he said with a grin, his eyes washing over her soft, flushed face. "Did you make them, Persephone?"

"Yes."

"And some mushrooms in hemlock gravy?" he teased.

She smiled at him. "Only as a side dish," she replied.

His eyes held hers, narrowing, glittering, as the smile left his mouth. His big hands tightened on her waist in a hungry, painful grip.

"Why don't you turn around?" he murmured in a deep, lazy tone. "I'd rather taste you than the canapes."

She blushed to the roots of her hair.

"I...I have to finish these," she protested breathlessly, tugging at his big, warm hands.

His open mouth ran up and down the softness of her neck in a sensuous, slow caress. "You smell of spring buds opening after a soft gray rain. No heavy perfume. No stiff hairspray and layers of makeup. You make me hungry, wood nymph."

She drew a deep, slow breath. "Would you like another canape?" she asked, trying to make a joke out of it.

"Come outside with me," he murmured at her ear, his teeth lightly nipping the lobe, "and let me make love to you."

"Mr. Devereaux!" she whispered shakily.

Soft, deep laughter was muffled against her neck. "You sound like an outraged virgin, something we both know damned well you're not. Stop pretending."

She strained at his imprisoning hands. "Whatever I am is none of your business!" she spat over her shoulder. "Let me go!"

He started to say something but the door

opened behind them and a silky voice purred, "Adrian, if you're quite through marking time with the hired help, I'd like to dance."

He turned gracefully for such a big man, his head tilted at an arrogant angle while he eyed the small blond intruder. "Meredith is my secretary," he said slowly, deliberately, "not 'hired help' as you so delicately put it. Watch those claws, little cat, or I'll trim them off to the quick!"

Behind him, peering around that broad, muscular shoulder, she saw Fayre's face go white with the shock of his cold fury. "I...I didn't mean..." she stammered.

"Get out." He said it without ever raising his voice, but the impact was just as visible.

"Excuse me," Fayre said weakly and turning, with a small accusing glance at Adrian, went back to where the music was throbbing in a disco beat.

Adrian lit a cigarette and stood with his back to her for several seconds before he turned. His dark eyes scanned her face quietly.

"You attack me all the time," Dana murmured, working again on the tray. "Why shouldn't she?"

"Because," he explained simply, "nobody touches you except me. In any way. Nobody."

She met his level gaze and felt something inside her tremble at the dark intensity of it. It was as if he'd reached out and marked her for life, a possession that was non-physical but permanent.

"Let Lillian finish that," he said suddenly, crushing out his fresh cigarette in an ashtray. "I've got plans for you."

"But..."

He put an iron hand behind her back and propelled her into the living room. The lights were low, the band was playing a slow, seductive tune, the assembled couples were wrapped around each other as they shuffled their feet lazily to the beat. Nervously, Dana looked for Fayre and found her smiling up at a man a little older than Adrian, darting an icy glance Dana's way.

Before that warning glitter had time to

register, Dana found herself imprisoned in Adrian Devereaux's big, warm arms, locked to his broadness as he drew her along in a slow rhythm.

"Don't be so damned conventional," he murmured, and, catching her hands, moved them into the thick cloud of hair on his chest. "You're not a baby."

She swallowed nervously, and tried to draw a deep breath. "I…I haven't danced in a long time."

"Obviously." One big, manicured hand came up to cover her cold one where it lay uneasily on his warm body. He pressed it into the mat of hair. "Your hands are like ice."

"It…it's a little…chilly," she faltered, drowning in the feel of his powerful, sensuous masculinity, the musky fragrance of his cologne, the strength of his arms.

His breath, whiskey scented, filled her nostrils as he lowered his forehead against hers. "God, you're soft," he breathed deeply. "Like silk where you touch me." His fingers came up and brushed against her chin shifting her face against his shoulder so that he could look down into her confused, soft eyes. His gaze dropped to her parted, pink mouth. Incredibly, he started to bend his head and she buried her face against him, the hair on his chest tickling her soft skin, the heavy thud of his pulse like distant drums in her ear.

His arms tightened around her. "Come outside with me," he whispered sensuously.

"No!" she replied huskily. "P...please, I don't know what kind of game this is, but I...I don't want to play it! If you have to punish me, can't you do it...some other way?! Why must you be so cruel!"

He stopped in his tracks and looked down at her. The tenderness went out of him in a flash of black eyes and he released her so suddenly she almost staggered.

Without another word, he turned away and made a beeline for Fayre, taking her away from her partner and jerking her against his body. Fayre caught Dana's eyes as the younger woman started back to the kitchen, and there was triumph in her sharp features.

The confrontation was inevitable from the very beginning, and Dana had expected it. But the venom in Fayre's face was still enough to paralyze her instantly when the little blonde tore into her bedroom as she was getting her shawl and preparing to leave.

"He belongs to me," she told Dana without preliminaries, her cold eyes summing up the taller woman in one insulting glance. "I've held him longer than any of the others, and I've got my eye on a wedding ring. Don't think you're going to cut me out, honey. It'll take more than a skinny little innocent like you to do that. Hands off. You understand?!"

Dana eyed the bleached blonde with a schooled calmness that came from years of dealing with hot tempers in city council chambers and county commission meetings.

"I don't believe in possession," she replied. "Not of things, or people. I work for Mr. Devereaux. Period. He wouldn't have me on a bet, and the feeling is mutual. If you don't believe me, ask him."

"Don't worry, I will." She threw the shawl around her shoulders. "Cool, aren't you?"

"I'm a reporter. We have to be."

"A reporter?!" A harsh, mocking laugh flared out of that slender throat. "And he hired you? Why, it was a woman reporter who ruined him…!"

"It was me." Dana said it deliberately and saw the confusion in the other's expression.

"Vengeance?" Fayre sighed. "I can almost feel sorry for you. Almost. But whatever his reasons for hiring you, just remember he's committed. Body and soul," she added deliberately. She turned and left the room with a trail of Chanel drifting behind her.

Dana mumbled something under her breath and slammed the bedroom door after the woman's retreating figure. She stayed there for the rest of the night, even refusing a final cup of coffee with Lillian.

*   *   *

The atmosphere was frigid for days after the party. Dana took dictation and planned her employer's appointments and kept his calendar with the absolute minimum of conversation. She took her meals in the kitchen with Lillian and kept out of his way every minute she could. He noticed this, and it did nothing for his black mood.

Three days in New York didn't improve him, either. He stood over Dana in the den, his eyes on the appointment calendar she was making an addition to, his mouth a thin line.

"Hold it," he said shortly. "You're scheduling me for the Chamber of Commerce banquet on the twenty-seventh. I won't be here," he added, one long, darkly masculine finger touching hers on the calendar to point out a scrawl in one corner. "I've got a meeting with Callahan and Vaughan on that new equipment I'm ordering."

"I'm sorry," she said quietly, feeling his breath in her hair as he leaned over her. "I didn't see that."

"Did you bother to look?" he asked harshly.

"Yes, sir, I did," she defended herself weakly. She laid the calendar aside and stood up, moving away from him.

"Where the hell do you think you're going?" he demanded.

"To…to help Lillian get supper on the table."

"My God, how did she ever manage to do it without you?" he growled, glaring at her across the room. "All right, run, Meredith. You'll eventually wear yourself out."

She had her hand on the doorknob and was just about to open it.

"Meredith."

"Yes, sir?"

"When you're through pecking at your supper, come back in here. I've got to work up a report on our latest production schedules."

"Yes, sir."

She dreaded those minutes alone with him, and her appetite dropped again.

Lillian grimaced at the food she left on

the plate. "You're going to blow away if you don't start eating!" she scolded.

Dana managed a wan smile. "All the way back to Miami, do you think?" she laughed mirthlessly. "I...I left someone there I'm concerned about. I can't even call to find out..."

"And why not?" Lillian was indignant. "You aren't a prisoner here, and the Mister wouldn't begrudge you a phone call."

"Lillian, he begrudges me the air I breathe," she said miserably, "Speaking of which, I've got to go back in there and take some dictation. I thought I heard the TV."

"You did. He's watching it." Lillian smiled at the shock on Dana's face. "Oh, he does, occasionally. Some cable movie, I think. It should be just about over by now. He had a tray in there."

"I set him a place in the dining room."

"One man, all alone, in that huge room?" Lillian asked gently. "Would you eat in there?"

The thought shocked her. Was he vulnerable enough to be lonely? She'd never considered it before, and it touched her in some unfamiliar way.

She knocked gently at the door of the study and went in, closing it behind her.

"Just a minute, Persephone, it's almost over. Sit down," he said over his shoulder. He was leaning forward on the couch, his eyes glued on the screen, not noticing that Dana came no closer to the wide-screened color TV.

She stood with her back against the cold wood of the door, trembling from one end of her body to the other, her horrified eyes hypnotized by the sight of a dam bursting on the TV screen, spreading a watery blanket of death over screaming victims. Her legs felt as if they were going to collapse under her. Her throat dried up. It was only six months ago and she was seeing her nightmares in full color.

With a terrible effort, she closed her eyes and felt the shudder rip through her, while the sound of the rushing water pounded in her ears and brought the old tears washing down her face. "Let it end, let it end, let it end," she chanted silently like a prayer, "let it end. God, let it end!"

Five

Seconds later, mercifully, a commercial took the place of the flood scene.

"Not bad, for a disaster flick, was it?" Adrian asked as he snapped off the television. "Well, let's get to..." He stopped in mid-sentence, looking at her where she was frozen, white-faced and trembling.

With an effort, she straightened and dashed the tears away impatiently. "My...my pad's on the desk," she whispered huskily, moving toward it.

He intercepted her, his big hands catching her head to tilt her flushed, tear-stained face up to his dark, narrow eyes. "What's the matter?" he asked gently.

"It…it's nothing, really," she said with a hollow laugh.

He scowled, darting a glance at the black television screen as his eyes came back to capture hers. "The movie? My God, honey, I didn't think…" he said harshly.

Her eyes widened, the question in her whole look.

"Yes, I know," he said, confirming her suspicions. "Charlie told me all about it. My God, little girl, why didn't you say something?"

"What should I have said?" she asked bitterly. "Please don't look at any movies with dambursts in them, or listen to any recordings that sound like rushing water because they give me hysterics? Don't take me to a waterfall, because I'll scream when I hear the water?" She laughed shakily. "Right after it happened, I couldn't take a bath, do you know, because the water sounded...God, I can't! I can't think about it, please...please, let's get to work, please..."

He drew her gently against him, his arms swallowing her up, warm and powerful and almost tender. "Tell me about it. Tell me everything you remember."

"I...I can't...bear to remember!" she wept, shuddering.

"Until you let it out," he said quietly, "it's going to haunt you like a ghost. Meredith, you don't face problems by running from them, haven't you learned that in your young life?"

She lifted her face to his. "I don't run from much, Mr. Devereaux," she reminded him proudly.

A wisp of a smile curved his broad, hard mouth. "Don't you, Persephone?"

"If I have to qualify it, only from devils," she replied.

"*Deh-vuls*, did you say?" he asked, his eyes dark and laughing.

"You needn't make fun of my accent," she returned. "You have one of your own!"

"Me?" He scoffed at that. "Not a trace."

"Say card. Go ahead, I dare you," she challenged, the flood forgotten in the business of arguing with her dark enemy.

"Card," he said, lifting his head arrogantly.

"Aha, you see?!" she burst out, her eyes gleaming with laughter, her small hands pressing quickly against his broad chest.

"See what?" he asked.

"You say 'cahd'," she explained impatiently.

He chuckled softly. His dark eyes traced the lines of her cheeks, her mouth, her nose. "You'd rather fight me than eat, wouldn't you?" he asked deeply. "I liked that about you three years ago, I recognized a kindred spirit. Do you believe in reincarnation, Meredith? That we take an instant like, or dislike, to a stranger because we knew him or her in another lifetime?"

"I don't know," she admitted. "Some

people...some places...it's like going home when you're around them.''

"Isn't it, though?" he asked in a soft, low tone.

She felt her pulse race at the look in his dark eyes and abruptly turned away. "I'll get my pad."

"Do that," he said with a lightning change back to his normal curtness. "I could use a few hours sleep. These damned cross-country jaunts are getting to me.''

"Old age creeping up?" She couldn't resist it, darting a glance at him from under her lashes.

His bold, slow eyes touched her from head to toe.

"Come upstairs with me, you impudent little taffy cat, and I'll show you how old I am," he replied in a tone that brought the blood burning into her cheeks.

"Uh...I'm ready when you are," she said, side-stepping the innuendo as she dropped into the chair at his desk with her steno pad in her lap and her pen ready.

"Oh?" Both dark eyebrows went up

and she felt herself cringing in the chair as what she'd said echoed in her mind. "A Freudian slip?"

With a glimmer of the old Dana Meredith, she peeked under the hem of her skirt and shook her head. "Nylon," she corrected.

He threw back his head and laughed like the devil he was, and she couldn't bite back a giggle of her own. The years and arguments and bitterness fell away, and she was his secretary and he was her boss, and it was like the sun coming up in the morning.

"Shut up and write, you little monster," he chuckled. "Ready? Production figures on the cutting room..."

She lay awake for a long time, watching the moon-washed pattern of leaves dance on the coverlet of her bed. If she'd had anything to make her sleep, she'd have taken it. The movie brought it all back, and it was taking her forever to push it far enough away.

Far away in the darkness, there was a

sound. A rumble, vaguely like thunder, above the steady beat of the rain. Then a crashing watery roar seemed to come out of nowhere. On a wide plain, she was standing, paralyzed, watching, as a thirty foot wall of muddy, debris-carrying water came tumbling over the waterfall and down over houses and trees. Frightened into action, she turned and ran, her thin white silk gown flaring out behind her as she sprinted ahead of the water, her lungs bursting, her legs stretched to the limit, and all around her the screaming, dying sound of victims being sucked into that wet, hungry maw…it caught her, and soaked her, and she was being dragged under…

"Meredith!"

The voice was salvation, shelter. It jerked her away in the nick of time, returning her to consciousness, bathed in sweat, tears rolling down her cheeks. She looked up drowsily into a broad, leonine face, its hard planes outlined in the light of her small lamp. He was sitting beside her on the bed, his eyes dark with concern, his big hand holding both of hers. He must have come running, she thought dazedly, because that broad, hair-riddled chest was bare, and all he had on were silk pajama bottoms.

"My God, I've never heard a scream like that," he said gently. "Are you all right, honey?"

"What?" she whispered, blinking her eyes, her breath coming in gasps, as if she'd been running.

His fingers brushed the damp, sweaty strands of her hair from her temples, her cheeks. "You had the great grandfather of all bloodcurdling nightmares, from the sound of it," he told her, a smile touching his hard mouth.

She swallowed, catching her breath, just his voice enough to calm her, to ease back to fear. "I'm all right," she whispered. "I'm all right, now."

"You were screaming," he said, his eyes narrowed. "I want you to tell me about it, Dana. Now."

It barely registered that he'd called her by her first name, or that the concern in those dark eyes was genuine. She didn't look higher than the bronzed skin of his throat.

"I can't."

"You can." He threw the covers back. His big arms lifted her, turned, cradled her until she was lying across his broad, warm chest with her cheek on his bare shoulder.

"Now," he murmured, looking down into her stunned eyes, caressing her bare shoulders, the soft curves of her nightgown, with gentle eyes. "Tell me what happened. Tell me what you saw. Nothing can hurt you, nothing can touch you as long as I've got you close like this. You're safe, honey. Tell me about it."

And she did. She told him about the dam that burst on a rainy Sunday morning in the darkness, and the unbelievable damage that a 30-foot wall of water can do to property and people, and about the victims...the victims...

"So many of them were children," she whispered, her face buried in the curling hair on his chest, her hands clinging to him. "So many...and the mud and mire was everywhere, and I didn't want to look. I didn't want to look!'' A sob shook her. ''But the whole place was covered with reporters and TV cameras and curiosity seekers who got past the rescue workers…! And that man, that poor harassed man in the thick of it trying to get his friend's body onto a stretcher past the television camera, and he said…he said…'' Her voice broke. ''He said we were vultures, that we were making a…a carnival out of it, and he was right, Adrian, we were, we were! All those poor, dead people, and the poor men who had to get them out and live with what they saw…!''

''Oh, my God,'' he breathed, his big arms swallowing her, protecting her. ''Oh, my God, Dana!'' She felt the powerful muscles go taut as he pressed her softness against him. His face buried itself in the thick, silky hair like a taffy cloud at her throat, holding her…just holding her.

''I felt so stupid, getting upset when all I had to do was write the story.'' She moved restlessly in his arms. ''But it hurt me. It hurt me! I've always been a little afraid of rivers and waterfalls, and I kept thinking how it must have been, all that water shooting down over the falls..."

His arms tightened even more, until her body was so close that his heartbeat shook it. "It's over," he murmured quietly. "All over. There's nothing to be afraid of anymore."

He rocked her gently, as if she were a child, and eased the fear and the trembling and the nightmarish memories. She felt her drawn muscles relaxing, felt the hardness of warm muscle and bone close against her in the drowsy silence that followed. She was aware of his warmth and strength, but even more aware of the sudden longing that flooded her yielding body. Only the thin slip of a nightgown separated flesh from flesh, and she could feel every hard line of his torso burning against hers. She was more aware than ever of his massive strength, of the raw power in that big body, of her own weakness.

"I...I'm all right now," she murmured, and gently pressed against that unyielding muscle.

"I'm not." He drew back a breath, and she could see the hard lines of his face, the strain in it, the tiny brown flames in his dark eyes. "I can feel every cell in your body through that gown, little girl," he said quietly, "every soft inch of you. I want you, Dana."

She tensed defensively, her eyes widening with fear.

"Don't go cold on me," he said, his big hand tracing shivery patterns along her throat, down to the neckline of her gown. "I'll be exquisitely gentle with you, little cat. I'll set you on fire and watch you burn in my arms..."

She drew up like a scorched leaf, turning her face away from that sensuous look in his eyes. "Please let me go," she pleaded tearfully. "I didn't know I was expected to pay for a shoulder to cry on."

She felt him stiffen, felt the anger touch every muscle in his vibrant body. "Payment in kind?" he growled. "At least you wouldn't have to buy me, Meredith, the way you had to buy that middle-aged..."

"You're middle-aged, too!" she threw

back at him, and regretted it instantly, even before she saw the explosion that blackened his glittery eyes.

"That," he said, his voice deep and dangerously soft, "was the biggest mistake you've made tonight." His hand tangled in her hair, jerking her face up to his, holding her head back against the merciless strength of his arm.

She stared back at him defiantly, determined not to show the fear that was ripping her pulse to shreds. "I'm not afraid of you," she said deliberately.

"Why should you be?" he asked carelessly. "I wouldn't be the first, and we both know it."

His eyes slid over her with an intimacy that made her blood surge in her veins. Like some magnificent dark illusion, he studied her, his dark hair rumpled, his eyes intense, his mouth almost smiling.

"Are you going to fight me, Meredith?" he asked in a slow, gentle tone.

Her lips trembled uncertainly, but she stood her ground. "To the last breath," she assured him.

His hand propelled her face up to his. His warm, chiseled lips parted hers with all a lover's practiced skill, smothering her protests as he forced her down into the pillows, his hard chest pinning her under him while he taught her how intimate a kiss could be.

With a sob, she fought him, panic making her wild as she struggled away from his deep, penetrating kiss and felt his bristly cheek rasp her swollen mouth.

He drew back, scowling down at the shock and fear that had left her face white.

"Meredith..." He murmured her name quietly, thoughtfully.

She sobbed, the sound pitiful in the darkness, like a child being whipped.

Abruptly, he let her go and stood up, his eyes puzzled, and anger mixed with it so that his face was frightening.

"Have you ever thought of going on the stage?" he asked with icy sarcasm. "You play the innocent with a flair. But you needn't bother, little cat. As you so accurately put it that night in the garden, it wouldn't mean anything." His eyes summed up her cowering body with a flick of indifference.

"That…wasn't how you sounded a minute ago," she choked.

One dark eyebrow went up. "Any woman can stir a man, Meredith."

She flushed darkly. "You needn't think I…was trying to…to stir *you*!" she cried.

He studied her through narrowed eyes, his face hard and impassive. "You're a puzzle, little one," he murmured quietly.

"What do you want from me?" she asked through the tears. "Please, Mr. Devereaux, what do you want from me?"

"What did Pluto want from Persephone?" he replied narrowly.

She closed her eyes wearily. "Please go away," she whispered. "Oh, please, go away."

"You prefer the nightmares to me, Meredith?" He moved to the door and paused to look at her. "Sometimes, little taffy cat, reality can be hell enough."

She heard the door close softly, and buried her face in the cool cotton pillow, weeping like a lost child.

* * *

She did her chores in a daze the next morning, the combination of the nightmare and her argument with Adrian leaving her drained and hollow-eyed.

"Won't you at least have a piece of toast?" Lillian coaxed when the pale girl refused breakfast.

"I'm sorry," she murmured with a smile, 'I'm just not hungry. I'll…"

The sudden insistent jangle of the telephone cut her off. She answered it automatically in the hall, preparing herself mentally for any one of a hundred situations it might mean.

"Dana, is that you?" came a familiar voice on the other end of the wire.

"Jack!" She broke into a smile. "Jack, is it you? How are you?!"

"I'm fine, honey, just fine. Dana…I've got some news for you."

It could only mean one thing, and she felt suddenly numb from her head down. "What is it?" she asked quickly.

"It's Katy," he said gently. "They transferred her from the nursing home to the hospital about an hour ago. Massive cerebral hemorrhage. You'd better come on down, honey. I'm sorry I had to be the one to call, but I told the doc it would be better coming from me. You okay?''

She felt her world collapsing around her. Massive hemorrhaging. That could mean... Her lips trembled on the words. ''I'll...I'll get on the...uh...the next flight. Where is she?''

''Sunnyside General. Dana, I'm sorry.''

''So...so am I. Thank you for calling, Jack. I'll be there...just as soon as I can, okay?''

''Sure. Take care.''

She nodded and laid the receiver back in the cradle. Her body shook with a hard sob. She sank into a chair by the telephone, just as the front door opened and Adrian came through it. It was odd for him to be home in the middle of the morning, but just the sight of him was enough to calm her.

''I forgot the Amhurst file,'' he said shortly. He shot a lightning glare at her tear-stained face. "Crying again? You're a damned watering pot lately."

"Please, I have to...to go to Miami," she said unsteadily. "Right away."

"Why?"

"My mother's in the hospital," she choked, forcing her voice to be calm. "Stroke. A massive one. Please, I need to see about...about reservations and..."

"Nice try, honey," he said coolly, "but it's a little trite. No, Persephone, you're not going to Miami to see your lover just yet. I've got plans for you."

He turned away and started into his den. "It's the truth!" she cried, her white face as chalk. "Oh, God, I'm not lying. You've got to believe me. I'm telling you the truth!"

"It would be a famous first," he said carelessly, not even slowing down as he went through the door. "Coming from you, the truth would be worthy of a celebration."

"She may die!" she wept, the tears streaming down her face. "I have to go!"

His dark eyes met hers, and she'd never

seen them so cruel. "Then I'll let you go to the funeral. Get to work, Meredith, I don't pay you for cheap hysterics. You aren't going to escape me that easily."

With a broken sob, she turned and ran into the library, locking the door after her. What could she do? Run away? She didn't have the air fare, he hadn't paid her, and her bank account was almost bare. She pushed the wild hair away from her eyes and studied the phone on the writing table. Jack. She could call Jack and have him call Adrian... A long shot, but worth a try, she had to go, she had to!

She picked up the receiver with trembling hands and dialed the number direct, her nerves screaming as she waited for the call to be transferred to the newsroom, and then waited for Jack to answer. It seemed to take forever.

An eternity later, Jack's deep voice came on the line. "Hello?"

"Jack..." her voice broke and she struggled to get it back. "Jack, I've got a...a problem and I need help. My...Mr. Devereaux won't listen, he thinks I'm lying…oh my God, please…Jack, talk to him, please talk to him. I've got to go to Miami!!'' A sob shook her slender body, ending on a gasp of pure anguish. ''Please, please…!''

''I'm here,'' said a voice on the extension, deep and utterly quiet. ''That you, Jack? What the hell's going on?''

She heard Jack explaining through a fog of emotion. Gently, she hung the phone up and sat down in the chair at the writing table with her face in her hands, weeping as if her heart would break.

Minutes later she heard the doorknob rattle. ''Dana, open the door.''

She was spurred into motion by the authority in that deep, strange voice. She opened the door, but looked no higher than his white crisp collar.

''I'll…pay you…back for the call,'' she managed brokenly.

His big hands caught in her hair, pulling her face against him. His broad chest rose and fell in a hard, heavy sigh. ''Oh, God, I'm so sorry,'' he whispered gruffly.

The words shocked her. She'd never

heard him apologize for anything, not ever. "I...I want to go home," she choked.

He drew a handkerchief from his pocket and tilted her face up to his so he could wipe away the tears.

"Go upstairs and pack what you need for a few days," he said gently. "I'll call and make the reservations. Are you all right?"

She barely registered the concern in his dark eyes, the tenderness in the big hand that was mopping up her face. "I'm fine."

"Like hell you are," he replied. "Wash your face. It'll help. Can you be ready in thirty minutes?"

She nodded.

"Move, Persephone."

She went up the stairs with his handkerchief clutched in her nerveless fingers. Packing took only minutes. She hardly saw what she was doing, and it was only due to Lillian's sudden appearance that any shoes, stockings or nightclothes were included. The older woman helped her gather everything together and then led her downstairs with a comforting arm around her thin shoulders.

Adrian was standing at the front door, waiting for Frank, who was tucking a suitcase into the boot of the Lincoln. "Give me your case, I'll have Frank load it," he said without preamble, taking it from her cold hands.

"Have a safe trip," Lillian told her. "God bless."

Impulsively, Dana kissed her wrinkled cheek and turned to go out the door.

The trip to the busy airport was a blur. Adrian was quiet, and Dana withdrew into the past, into memories of the way her life had been just years ago, before her father's death had triggered so much tragedy.

In her mind, she could see Katy Meredith in the old days, a sparkling dark-eyed jewel with a vitality, a love of life that burned like a candle in a chapel. Katy, laughing as she played hostess at political gatherings, chaired fund drive committees, played golf...

She felt something warm and strong against the coldness of her fingers where they lay on the seat of the car. Her eyes glanced at them and saw Adrian's big, dark hand swallow the coldness and warm it.

"I...I'll come back," she said quietly. "I don't know when..."

"I'm going with you."

She met his dark, level gaze. "Why?"

His fingers gripped hers closely. "Who else have you got, Meredith?" he asked.

Tears welled in her eyes and a sob broke from her lips. She turned away, watching the blur of passing traffic.

"Do you want me to hold you?" he asked in a strange, soft murmur.

She glanced up at him, saw the tenderness in his eyes... "W...would you?" she whispered.

His gray jacket came open against his white shirt as he reached for her, drawing her slender body against him, easing her cheek onto his warm, hard chest.

His fingers tangled slowly, gently in her loosened hair. "It's going to be all right," he said, brushing her temple with his lips. "It's going to be all right, my baby."

She closed her eyes and relaxed with a trembling sigh. He was warm and strong, and it was so good to lean on someone just this once, to have the security of someone else making decisions, leading the way. And in spite of all he'd said, and all he'd done, loving him was a way of life. Even through the fear and the pain and the grief, being in his arms was a balm worth any wounding.

The flight seemed short. In no time Adrian had her off the plane and into a rented car. The first thing he did was check them into adjoining rooms at a hotel near the hospital. Dana had had to give up her small apartment when she went to Atlanta, so the hotel rooms were a necessity.

She had time to change her dress and compose herself before they went to the hospital. She clung to his hand all the way up the four floors and all the way down the hall to her mother's semi-private room. But she hesitated at the door, trembling all over.

His fingers meshed with hers, palm to palm, strong and reassuring. "Face it," he said quietly. "I won't leave you."

Six

Two beds were close together in the small room, but only one of them was occupied. A thin, wraith-like little body was outlined by the crisp white hospital sheets and the single yellow blanket. An I.V. was hooked into the blue veins of the hand, and there was an oxygen mask around the nose. The small oval face was like old parchment, the big eyes closed, the mouth purplish.

"Oh, Mama," Dana whispered, unaware that she'd even spoken.

Adrian's hand tightened. He went with her to the bedside. "How long has she been like this?" he asked.

"Bedridden, you mean? For the past three years," she said quietly. "I moved her to Miami because I knew a specialist here who was willing to work with her."

There was a long, static silence.

"What kind of shape are you in financially, Meredith?" he asked.

"That's none of your…" she protested.

"Oh, hell, yes it is," he replied shortly, his eyes dark and unblinking as they met hers. "Tell me!"

She turned her attention back to Katy Meredith, haunted by the sight of her. She reached down and touched the frail arm. Pride fought with fatigue, and fatigue won. "My father was killed in an accident, over three years ago—just before I…started to work for you. He was heavily in debt, although Mama and I didn't know it at the time. He was her world, he was all the color and light in her life. When he died, she had the first of several strokes. They left her like this. It took everything, all the insurance money...everything, just to pay the debts and start paying on the hospital bills. Mama didn't have any hospitalization insurance.'' She drew in a sharp breath. ''I used to hear it said that everyone has a price. I found out then what mine was. I agreed to that masquerade, to get that story on you because there was nothing in the bank and I couldn't bear even the thought of charity. That man in the restaurant with me...he was our attorney. The check I was giving him was one I'd received from the insurance company on a policy I didn't even know Daddy had. It was a Godsend, that check. It made it possible to move Mama here. Afterwards, I was able to get a job with Charlie's paper and take over the bills.''

Adrian studied the frail little body on the bed. His face was like carved rock. ''How do you manage the nursing home on your salary?''

She shrugged. ''Frugally,'' she said with a wan smile.

''Without government assistance, too, right, Persephone?'' he asked curtly.

"She's not old enough to qualify, if looks are any indication."

"I made my own clothes, and kept a tight budget, and I lucked out on an apartment in a home with some very nice people." She closed her eyes. "From a Mercedes to a city bus and a two-story town house to a one-room efficiency…it was a long way down, and if it hadn't been for Dad's insistence that I take journalism courses, I don't know how we'd have survived."

"I don't see how the hell you are surviving," Adrian said in a cutting voice. "And she doesn't need to be in a semiprivate room. She damned well needs a round-the-clock nurse as well."

She glared at him. "Need has to adjust to ability," she reminded him.

"Why didn't you tell me this before?" he asked.

"Would you have listened, Mr. Devereaux?" she ground out.

He met her challenging look evenly. "My name is Adrian. Don't ever put a mister in front of it again. Sit down. I'll be back in a few minutes. Can I bring you a cup of coffee?''

It sounded like absolute heaven. She could almost taste it. "Oh, please!"

He left the room, and Dana was alone with the fragile fleshy shell of her mother. She sat down beside the bed, her eyes scanning the pronounced cheekbones, the sharp eyebrows, the thick, long eyelashes that had never needed mascara. There was nothing of the brown sparkle of those eyes that had loved life, nothing of the active woman whose endurance and vivacity were a watchword.

Dana laid her fingers on the cold, unmoving hand spread out on the white sheet. "I love you, Mama," she whispered.

But the lilting voice that had always answered her as a child answered her no more.

An hour later they left the hospital. Adrian had given the hotel number to the nurses' station and the business office, assuming the responsibility with customary nonchalance.

He propelled her toward the hotel restaurant firmly.

"Please, I can't eat anything," she protested as he seated her at a table in the cozy, dimly lit room. Red candles glowed softly against the stark white of the tablecloth.

"You've got to," he said matter-of-factly, seating himself across from her. "I talked to the doctor."

Her heart froze. "And...?"

A muscle in his jaw twitched. "I think you already know, honey. I think you knew when Jack called you. It's just a matter of time. Minutes. Hours. A few days. There's nothing more they can do. You know that, don't you?"

Tears welled in her eyes. She caught her lower lip in her teeth and stared at the tablecloth. She nodded silently.

The waitress came and Adrian ordered coffee and steaks and a salad for them. The waitress left, and he leaned back in his chair to light a cigarette, studying Dana through the smoke.

"I'm having her moved to a private

room," he said. "And I've engaged 'round the clock nurses. She won't be alone for a minute."

"But...!" she began, torn between wanting the best for Katy, and being unable to pay for it.

"We'll talk later. Right now, I'm going to feed you. Then you're going to lie down and rest for an hour or so. We'll go back to the hospital tonight, when you're rested."

"Are you going to tuck me in and give me a bottle, too?" she asked, irritation rising to camouflage the grief.

A tiny smile tugged at his hard, sensuous mouth. "Would you like me to?" he asked pointedly.

She felt her cheeks catch fire. The waitress came back just in time to save her from a reply.

That day set the pattern for the two that came after it. Adrian was with her almost every minute, only leaving her alone at bedtime. He propelled her from one place to another, propped her up, made her eat, stayed by the bedside with her. He was her mind for those horrible, cold days of impotent waiting, her consciousness, her guiding hand. And when the end came, quietly, at the end of a long, gray afternoon, he took her gently into his big arms and held her while she cried.

She sat on the edge of the bed that night, her eyes wide open, her heart aching as she remembered the still little form under the sheets, the doctor's comforting voice.

Adrian made arrangements for Katy to be taken back to Atlanta. In the morning, the hearse would come to take Katy Meredith home. In the morning, Dana would fly home with Adrian. In the morning...

But it was still night, and the first night she'd had to live with the loneliness of having no family left. And tears streamed down her pale cheeks as she sat there in her lace-trimmed brief nylon slip, her taffy-colored hair cascading around her shoulders in brilliant disarray.

She heard the door open and saw Adrian through a mist. He was still dressed, in well-fitted brown slacks and a white shirt open at the throat. His thick dark hair was rumpled, his face heavily lined, his eyes shadowed and quiet. He needed to shave; there was a faint hint of beard on his broad, leonine face. But all in all he was the most attractive man she'd ever known. He was so good to look at...

It took her a full minute to realize that she wasn't dressed. She started to get up and go after the robe at the foot of the bed, suddenly nervous, but he blocked her way.

"It's a little late for false modesty between us, Meredith," he said quietly. "I've seen you in a hell of a lot less."

"I...I know, but..." she murmured, feeling those dark, bold eyes run up and down her slenderness.

His big hands caught her shoulders gently. "I want you to forget convention for tonight. I want you to trust me in a way you've never been asked to trust a man before."

"What do you mean?" she asked weakly, looking no higher than the buttons on his shirt, pearly white buttons that were partially undone so that the hair-covered muscles were tantalizingly displayed. He smelled of tobacco and tangy cologne, and he was warm. Big and warm and solid.

"I want you to sleep with me."

Shocked, her red-rimmed eyes met his, asking questions her mouth couldn't shape.

He studied her face, her paleness, with a tenderness she never expected to see. "No strings, little taffy kitten," he said gently. "I'm offering you a shoulder to pillow your head, and an arm to hold you when the hurting breaks through that mask you wear. You're not going to close your eyes as long as you're alone in here, now, are you?"

"No," she admitted with a reluctant sigh. "Adrian, I...I really don't want to be alone," she added in a whisper. "But I..."

"I may be a devil, Persephone," he murmured deeply, "but I'm not quite a monster. Seduction in these circumstances would be beneath most men."

She met his eyes and read them. When he reached out and took her hand, she followed him back into his own room. He closed the connecting door and switched out the top light, leaving only the bedside lamp to light the way.

Turning back the covers, he put her under them and stretched himself out on top of them, drawing her close so that she could pillow her head on his broad, powerful shoulder.

"All right?" he asked gently.

"Yes, thank you," she murmured, feeling the tension slowly drain out of her as her drawn muscles relaxed. The strain of the past days caught up with her all at once, and she felt suddenly drowsy.

"Adrian, how old were you when your mother died?" she asked, her voice muffled against his warm shirt front.

"Ten," he said.

"Is that why your father took you on hunting trips with him...to make up for it?" she asked gently.

"Probably."

She nuzzled her cheek against the warm hardness of his chest. "Adrian, you're such a blabbermouth," she added with just a bit of her old cheek.

Soft, deep laughter shook the hard pillow under her ear. "Am I?" he taunted, and she felt his lips brushing her forehead.

Her fingers toyed with the button on his shirt as the drowsiness washed over her like warm bathwater. "I've got nobody now," she whispered, feeling the ache come back.

His big arms tightened, protectively, possessively. "Haven't you, Persephone?"

"Adrian."

"Hmm?" he murmured against her hair.

"What finally happened in the legend? Did Pluto let her go?" she asked on a yawn.

"I don't remember, honey. He was stubborn as all hell. I don't imagine he'd have set her free without putting up a fight—not if he cared as much as the legends say he did."

"That's funny."

"What is?"

"The devil caring about anyone," she explained. "Maybe he just had a good public relations department back then. Some old salt of a reporter who didn't get to heaven and had to earn a living some-how…"

He chuckled. "Go to sleep, little one."

"I don't usually sleep with men, you know," she murmured sleepily.

"This is a first for me, too, Meredith," he said with a trace of amusement in his deep, clipped voice. "I don't usually *sleep* with women."

"You ought to get more rest," she told him lazily. "A man of your advancing years needs his sleep."

"Why, you damned little impudent…!"

She laughed softly. "Touchy."

"My God, you'd try the patience of a saint, do you know that?"

"But, then, we've already agreed that you're not one," she reminded him.

"Damn you." He said it on a ripple of laughter, his big hand catching her hair to jerk her face back on the shoulder that was pillowing it. His dancing dark eyes met hers, something sensuous and just faintly dangerous burning in them. "Baby girl, you're touching a match to straw, do you know that? It's not going to take much more." His other hand came up to brush her flushed cheek, his fingers lightly tracing her soft mouth. "Do you understand me, or do you want me to spell it out?"

She blushed. "I think it might be a very good idea if I go to sleep."

"So do I," he murmured softly. He pressed her cheek back against his hard chest and put both arms around her. "Goodnight, little one."

"Goodnight, Mr. Devil," she whispered impishly.

His fingers smoothed her flyaway hair. "Dana."

"Yes, sir?"

"Don't call me sir."

"No, sir."

"Dammit…!"

"What?" she asked, feeling reality fade in and out as blessed sleep began to claim her.

"Are you going to call Jack in the morning?"

She tried to focus her mind. "I'd like

to, if you don't mind. He was...he was very good to Mama, and to me.''

''I don't mind, honey.''

She burrowed closer. ''Adrian, she's better off, isn't she?'' she whispered, feeling the pain come back. ''Isn't she?''

''You know that already.'' He drew her up closer, cradling her, rocking her gently in his warm embrace. ''Now go to sleep. Just go to sleep. I've got you, and nothing can hurt you. Sleep, my...''

His voice faded into nothingness in her mind.

She called Jack and had him meet them for breakfast at the hotel before they left. She was calmer now, the mask firmly in place over her raw emotions, coping.

''I'll never be able to thank you enough,'' she told him while Adrian went to pay the check. ''Never.''

Jack looked vaguely embarrassed. He fingered his coffee cup. ''You know when you come back, your job'll be waiting, don't you?'' he asked. He darted a glance toward Adrian's broad back at the counter.

"Meanwhile, maybe he'll keep your mind busy. You needed a break before. You need it even worse now. This business can be hell without periodic absences."

She managed a smile for him. "The phone rings and it's for him, now. I'm enjoying that. Nobody calls me to tell me about bank robberies. Or threatens to blow up my car. Except him," she added with a hint of a grin.

"He isn't what I expected," Jack said.

"What did you expect?" she asked.

"We'll go into it another time. Say, remember that flying saucer nut I was having fits with when you were here?"

She nodded. "Don't tell me he got kidnapped by little green men?"

"He says he did. Had the wire services all over us last week," he laughed. "You'd have loved it."

"Loved what?" Adrian asked, rejoining them.

"A story I was telling her," Jack grinned. "The newsroom sure is quiet these days. I kind of like it. Phyl doesn't threaten to stock my pool with guppies and give my unlisted number to high school journalism students.''

''It was only once,'' Dana reminded him.

''He had friends,'' Jack recalled. ''All would-be poets. 'I hear the gut-pounding rhythm of the slippery slimy surf slobbering...' Remember, Miss Meredith?''

''This shy, retiring, dignified little girl?'' Adrian asked curiously. ''My God, I'd never have believed it. She's sedate and efficient, but I didn't realize she was that dangerous.''

''Sedate?'' Jack had the expression of a man who'd been hit between the eyes with a scoop of ice cream. ''Dana?''

Adrian studied her in a long silence. His eyes narrowed thoughtfully, and they didn't leave her as Jack launched into more reminiscing. It kept her from thinking, and that was what she needed most of all.

The graveside service was held at the small cemetery of a Methodist church out in the metropolitan area of northwest Atlanta. A rolling, green slope of land with trees and tiny bronze markers instead of tombstones. A prayer was said. The minister took her hand and murmured words of comfort. The few Miami staffers who'd flown up for the funeral patted her on the back. Jack hugged her. And it was over. Adrian hustled her into the back seat of the Lincoln and held onto her hand as if it were made of gold while Frank turned the big car and headed it for the manor.

Dana closed her eyes and felt the last of the tears easing away the grief. It was over. It was over.

Seven

The nights were long at first, and there were occasional tears when she let herself remember. But Adrian wasn't shouting at her so much anymore. Lillian was kindness itself, and the grief was slowly fading.

"What the hell is this?" Adrian asked late one afternoon, his leonine face scowling blackly at something he saw on his appointment calendar. He traced it with a long finger and glanced at Dana. "You've got me down for dinner with Mendolsen

Thursday night. You know I hate Mendolsen's guts, how the hell do you expect me to eat?"

"But, you said..." she protested.

"I said, I wanted to talk to him, not that I wanted to wine him, dine him, and sleep with him!" he returned. "Get me out of it."

"But, he's out of town until Thursday afternoon," she exclaimed, her slender hands going out in a gesture of impotence.

"Then call him Thursday afternoon."

"But..."

"If you 'but' me one more time..." he threatened darkly.

She sighed. "All right, I'll do it. But, if I were you," she added with a hint of her old self, "I'd look under my pillow before I laid down on it."

Both dark brows went up. "What am I supposed to find?"

"I won't say," she replied, turning away. "But if you hear a hissing, rattling sound..."

"I thought you were afraid of snakes."

"Only male snakes," she qualified,

"with blue eyes. Actually, I'm very fond of female snakes. Especially," she added with a grin, "when they're dead."

He threw back his head and roared. "My God, how did that newspaper survive you?"

"I'm very sedate, remember?" she reminded him.

"Sedate, hell, you're going to give me a nervous breakdown," he replied with a chuckle.

"Give?" She shook her head. "I charge for those." She flipped her steno pad shut. "Am I through for the night?"

"As far as I'm concerned, you are. I'm taking Fayre to a concert," he added, flashing a glance her way.

She kept her expression unruffled. "Then I think I'll have an early night. I've been on the phone all day."

"Like old times, wasn't it?"

"Yes." She sighed.

"Miss it?"

She nodded with a smile. "I've been doing it for a lot of years."

He frowned thoughtfully, one hand

jammed into his pocket. His eyes swept over her slender body, the youth that made her cheeks soft and flushed, gave the soft brightness to her eyes. "Honey," he said softly, "you haven't lived a lot of years."

The tone of his deep voice made ripples down her spine. "I...I have to..."

"...help Lillian," he finished for her in a harsh growl. "God, I know, don't you always. Go ahead!"

She left him standing there, wondering silently at the harsh whip of his voice.

She went to her room after dinner and spent several restless hours there, until the walls started to close in. She remembered some typing she'd left until morning, and decided to finish it. At least it would keep her mind from wandering to Adrian and the dragon...

Her long hair loosened, dressed in the royal blue jersey dress she kept for casual wear, she closed the door of the den behind her and settled down at the typewriter.

The big chair that swallowed Adrian's

husky form left plenty of room around hers. Her hands touched the leathery arms, feeling it grow warm under her fingers, and she leaned back, her mind full of Adrian. If only she was sophisticated, like Fayre, and bright and gay and desirable. If only she hadn't ruined him. If only he wanted something from her besides vengeance—but, she sighed, that was the only reason he was keeping her here, and she knew it. Even though he'd been kindness itself since her mother's death, she knew it was always there, nagging at his temper, causing those frequent periods when he sat and stared at her, his dark eyes burning in that broad face. She had to be on her guard every minute. He might even stoop to making her love him.... Her eyes closed as if in pain. What an unbearable punishment, to have him know how she really felt! It would give him the most malicious pleasure to chide her for it, to ridicule her, if he found out. Nothing, nothing, would be worse than that!

She gathered her hastily scribbled shorthand notes, and began to type.

She was so intensely involved in what she was doing that she didn't hear the disturbance outside, or the front door open, or the whisper of the den door as it slid open to admit a familiar dark, husky form.

He stood there for a moment, his eyes sliding over the silky long hair, the unguarded vulnerability of that young face, the slender, flowing curves of her body, so graceful in the way she sat. He leaned back against the door, his eyes soft in that instant; watching her like some great, dark cat might watch its prey unobserved.

Something, a tingling awareness, made her glance up. She jumped, seeing him there unexpectedly. "You startled me!" she gasped.

"You startled me the first time I ever saw you," he replied obscurely. He loosened his tie and pulled it off, tossing it to the couch. His fingers went to the buttons of his immaculate white shirt after he'd shed his jacket, unfastening it halfway down that massive dark chest with its covering of black hair.

"God, I'm tired," he murmured. He ran

a hand through his hair, rumpling it, and sank into the deep, soft armchair by the fireplace, crossing his legs. "I don't give a damn about Wagner, and I had to sit through a program of it that nearly drove me to drink. Do you like Wagner, Meredith?" he asked, pausing to light a cigarette before he looked at her.

She shook her head. "I like Debussy and Dvorak."

"The romantics." A smile touched his chiseled mouth. "I might have known."

"You don't like them, either, I suppose?" she fished.

He studied her quietly. "I like Debussy, Neil Diamond, Kenny Rogers, Rachmaninoff, Stravinsky, and Alice Cooper. Does that answer your question?"

She laughed softly and her eyes widened. "Alice Cooper?"

"Don't knock it, honey," he grinned. "Music is music, and I like it all."

"Really?" She darted a mischievous glance at him. "I thought you older people only liked waltzes and fox-trots."

"*Older* people?" He stood up, the cigarette smoking in his hand and moved lazily to the desk, perching himself on its edge beside her. "Would you care to elaborate?"

"Well," she replied, the proximity making her nervous, the scent of his expensive cologne drowning her in sensation, "you just don't look like a man who'd like hard rock," she replied.

One darkly masculine hand, with its sprinkling of hair, reached out and touched the curve of her throat, coaxing her face up. His eyes met hers, dangerous, deep, holding her gaze until she thought her heart would jump out of her chest.

"Your heart's racing," he murmured, his fingers playing havoc as they traced the throbbing vein in her neck.

"I... Is it?" she managed in a strange, husky voice.

He leaned down until his breath was whispering across her trembling mouth, until his dark eyes filled the room.

He drew back as she swayed helplessly toward him, chuckling like the devil he was. "Don't worry, little girl," he said softly, "I don't rob cradles." Taking a long draw from his cigarette, he stood up with a taunting smile at the nervous wreck he'd left in the chair before him. "Come on, Dana, let's get some coffee and cake. I barely touched my supper."

"C...coffee and cake?" she faltered.

"Aren't you hungry, honey?" he asked with one raised eyebrow. "God knows I am. Have coffee with me, at least."

"All right." She tugged her calm mask back in place, unaware of the mischief in the dark eyes she couldn't see, and followed him to the kitchen. That he wanted her company was enough to kindle a glow in the pit of her stomach.

She made coffee while he sat quietly at the kitchen table and watched her.

"I never thanked you," she murmured, pouring water into the automatic coffee maker.

"For what?"

"Going with me. Staying with me. Easing the hurt," she replied, glancing at him past the silky curtain of her long hair.

"I'd have done that for my worst en-

DIANA PALMER   143

emy, didn't you know?'' he asked with a hint of smile. His eyes narrowed. ''Don't credit me with too much compassion. I never make investments without a guaranteed return.''

''What did you get out of it, then, except a lot of expense?'' she asked. ''And I'm going to pay you back, every penny,'' she added firmly.

''You can work it out,'' he told her, not bothering to argue. He leaned back in the chair, his darkness, his broadness tantalizing in the silence and the privacy of the kitchen. Her eyes were drawn against her will to that spray of black hair peeking out of the unbuttoned white shirt, and she was remembering how it had felt under her hands that night she danced with him at the lake....

''You're staring, Persephone,'' he taunted.

Flushing, she drew her eyes back to the coffee maker. ''I wish you wouldn't call me that.''

''Why not? It fits.''

"You wouldn't like it if I called you Pluto."

"Damned straight, and I wouldn't advise you to try it. I like mine with cream," he added as she poured coffee into the two big, thick mugs. She paused to lace his with cream before she set it in front of him.

"You always pick on me," she protested, dropping into the chair across from him, vulnerable in the soft blue dress with her hair spreading like yellow satin onto her shoulders, her eyes huge and brown and wistful. "Why can't I hit back?"

"Honey, you've got a foolproof method for getting at me, and you don't even know it."

She stared at him blankly. "What?"

But he only shrugged. "Forget it." He sipped his coffee absently. "What were you doing up—waiting for me?"

She blushed furiously. It had never occurred to her that he might put that interpretation on it. "I...I just couldn't sleep," she hedged. "And I needed to finish that...all right, I was thinking about Mama and I needed something to do," she admitted finally, wearily.

"It passes, Dana," he said quietly. His fingers absently stroked the coffee mug. "I remember when Janine died..."

"Your...your wife?" she asked gently.

"My wife." He stared down into the shimmer of light that reflected in the deep mug. "It was a merger more than a marriage—her family had cloth mills, mine manufactured clothing. But I'd lived in the same house with her long enough to miss the scent of her perfume in a room, or the sound of her humming when she dressed for a night on the town." He chuckled. "God, I even missed the nylons she left strewn across the floor. Neatness wasn't one of Janine's better points. She was the unhappiest woman I ever knew. She laughed all the time, but her eyes died before she did."

"You loved her?"

He studied the softness in her eyes, the vulnerability. "At that point in my life, little girl, I didn't really know what love was." He watched her quietly, and there was in his expression something totally adult, masculine and provocative. "Dana, you're so very young," he said in a tone that made her blush.

"Try to burp me, and it's going to be a free-for-all in here," she warned quietly.

A swarthy grin cut across his face. "Honey, if I ever take you on my lap, it won't be to burp you."

She lifted her face defiantly, ignoring the heat in her cheeks. "You only just got through saying you don't rob cradles," she reminded him.

He chuckled softly. "I have to keep your age in mind. Occasionally I forget that you're eighteen years my junior."

"Seventeen," she corrected him. "I'll be twenty-three the day after tomorrow."

He held her eyes in the silence, looking his fill while her heart shook. "I was already a man when you were just born, Dana," he said gently.

Her gaze slid over the lines in his face, his broad, chiseled mouth, the darkness of his skin...touching it with her eyes. "Adrian..."

"What is it…something you're afraid to ask?" he mused. "I don't bite."

"Did you…I mean, most men…" she trembled over the words. "Did you ever want children?"

Something—brown sunlight, an explosion of autumn leaves, a burst of brown flame—touched those dark eyes and dilated them. "Why did you ask that?" he queried gently.

She dropped her eyes, afraid that he might see the answer. "I just wondered."

He put out the stub of his cigarette and finished his coffee. "You'd better get some sleep, little one. It's very late. No, leave the cups, let Lillian get them in the morning." He held the door open for her. "I never did get my cake."

"Oh, did I forget…Adrian, I can still cut you a slice—" she began.

"It's just as well," he replied, clicking off the light, "I'm heavy enough without it."

Impishly, she put out a slender hand and touched the hard muscle of his stomach above his belt. "You're big, not heavy," she teased.

He caught her hair and tugged her face up with a firm, steady pressure, moving closer so that she could feel the warmth of his body, so that the scent of him filled her nostrils.

"Come here," he murmured, and bent his head to touch his mouth very gently to hers in a kiss that brought the stars spinning down.

He drew away a heartbeat later, his face solemn, his eyes quiet. "Better than cake," he whispered deeply, and a slow, wicked grin touched his mouth. "No calories."

She managed to smile back and disengaged her hair from his hands. "Goodnight," she said, turning away to hide the effect that brief kiss had on her pulse.

"Dana?"

"Yes?" she replied without turning, at the foot of the staircase.

"I want children very much."

Stunned, she met his eyes, saw the dark gentle smile in them, and couldn't find words to answer him. She only nodded and turned away, curiously breathless.

The next afternoon, Dana was sealing a letter when the phone rang and a familiar deep voice came over the line.

"What are you doing?" he asked lazily, as if he had all the time in the world to talk to her.

"Getting out a letter, to that textile equipment company you wrote to about the buttonhole machines," she replied softly.

"Learning the textile business, are you? I'll have to take you through one of the plants. How about tomorrow? I'll take you to lunch first."

"A...all right," she murmured, taken aback at the invitation, at the caress in his deep voice. It was as if last night had lowered all the cold barriers between them.

"By the way," he added, "call Fayre and tell her I won't be able to make it tonight. I've got to fly up to South Carolina for a meeting. And get me a reservation on the next flight to Greenville."

"Yes, sir," she said absently, jotting down notes.

"Dana...!" he threatened.

"I...I mean, yes, I will," she replied quickly, omitting the "sir" this time.

"Behave, brat. I'll see you in the morning."

"Yes..." She stopped again, just in time.

"Try 'darling'," he suggested in that deep seductive tone he could use when he wanted something. "Later, honey."

The line went dead, and she sat there holding the receiver as if it were a fragrant rose, just looking at it for a long time afterwards.

Fayre was stunned by the news that Adrian wasn't going to take her to the ballet, and Dana caught the full weight of her disappointment.

"I don't see why he couldn't fly back tonight," she said icily. "We've had tickets for three months, it isn't as if he didn't know in time! What kind of meeting was it?"

"I don't know, Miss Braunns," Dana explained patiently, toying with her pencil. "He didn't tell me, and I didn't ask."

"Cute, aren't you? Did you make that appointment for him?" Fayre asked pointedly.

"To get him out of town, you mean?" Dana laughed shortly. "Miss Braunns, what he does is no business of mine except where my job is involved. I don't want to be here any more than I want to live in the Colombian jungles, but I don't have a choice. If you want to know why he isn't coming back tonight, you call him and ask him. For all I know, he may have two women…"

"How dare you?" Fayre spat. "Nobody talks to me like that!"

"Adrian does," Dana replied calmly.

There was a long, burning silence on the other end of the line, and she could feel her ears burn. "You little tramp," Fayre hissed. "I'll get you for that if it's the last thing I ever do. You're not cutting me out with Adrian…!"

Dana put the receiver down with a thud.

She found herself shaking with rage, with humiliation, with apprehension. This would just give Adrian another stick to beat her with. Why couldn't she keep her mouth shut? She sighed. Fayre would have irritated her anytime, anywhere—she was just naturally abrasive. But her relationship with Adrian made it worse. To think of that small, too-sweet face pressed against his dark, broad chest...

The phone rang. Hesitantly, she lifted the receiver, her heart thudding, expecting disaster in a deep, angry voice...

"Hello?" she murmured.

"Miss Meredith?" came the reply. "This is the Juliane Travel Service. I'm confirming your reservation on the flight to Greenville..."

She listened to the pleasant female voice with a tiny smile. Sometimes, heaven was kind.

The morning of her birthday started off backwards. She overslept and missed breakfast. The phone went wild the minute she walked into the office, and it was after ten a.m. when the rush finally stopped.

Lillian poked her head around the door. "I haven't been able to tell you—the Mister said Frank was to bring you to his office at eleven. Sorry, honey," she smiled. "It's been a busy morning, hasn't it?"

Dana smiled. "Very. I know what it's all about—he's taking me on a tour of his plant, one of them, anyway."

"Oh, is that it?" Lillian asked with a strange smile.

"Of course." Dana stood up. "I'd better start getting ready, I guess."

"Wear something pretty," Lillian said with a wink.

Adrian was waiting for her when she got off the elevator and stepped out onto the carpeted floor of the Devereaux Textile Corporation offices.

His dark eyes went up and down the soft sleeveless beige jersey dress that clung to her slender figure like a second skin, narrowing to the upswept hairdo that lent quiet elegance to the simple lines of the dress.

"Nice," he remarked quietly. "Are you hungry?"

She nodded. Her eyes darted around to the desks sitting outside the offices.

"I'll give you the two-dollar tour another time," he said, and took her elbow to lead her back into the elevator, ignoring the intense, curious stares his employees were giving the slender young woman at his side. "Do you like crepes?"

"Crepes? You mean, like strawberry crepes?" she asked, all eyes as she looked up at him in the cozy confines of the elevator.

He studied her in silence, his dark eyes sketching the soft lines of her face. "Little taffy kitten," he murmured gently.

She flushed, lowering her eyes to the deep polish of his shoes.

Soft, deep laughter drifted over her head. "Crepes can be a main course as well as a dessert, Meredith," he told her. "I'm going to take you to a creperie at Lennox Square for lunch."

"Lennox? But that's almost in Buckhead, have you the time...?" she exclaimed.

"The plant I'm taking you to see is on

the way," he told her. The elevator stopped and he stood to one side to let her out. "Besides," he added, "I have to pick up something at the jewelers."

"Oh," she murmured weakly. An apology present for the dragon, no doubt, for missing the ballet.

In the parking lot, he put her in the back seat of the sleek silver-gray Rolls and slid in beside her, leaving the traffic to Frank, who took it in stride.

Dana glanced at Adrian where he sat beside her, one big arm carelessly thrown over the back of the seat, his dark eyes watching her.

"Dana."

"Yes?"

His dark fingers stretched to touch the silky bun at the back of her neck. "Take it down."

"I…I thought it went well…with the dress," she faltered, his nearness, the dark sensuous look in his eyes making her tremble.

His fingers touched her cheek, her soft

mouth. "Take it down, sweetheart," he whispered.

The endearment made her pulse go wild. With shaking fingers she tugged out the hairpins and fumbled at the clasps, letting the long, silky length down around her shoulders. She dug a small brush out of her purse and trailed it through the taffy-colored strands. When she put the brush away, his fingers tangled gently in the loosened hair. "God, I love your hair," he murmured deeply, his eyes meeting hers in an intense stare.

She couldn't say a word. He was too close, too overwhelming at this range, with his hard, dark face filling the world.

He moved away abruptly with a hard sigh, his attention going to Frank. "How about some music, Frank?" he asked gruffly. "It's been one hell of a morning. I could use a little soothing."

"Nothing I caused, I hope?" she asked in a small voice, remembering Fayre.

He chuckled. "Fayre, you mean?" he asked with a knowing smile.

Blushing, she nodded.

"I can handle Fayre, little one. If she'd wanted to go to the damned ballet that much, she had the tickets and no shortage of prospective dates. I don't have any strings on her, and she doesn't have any on me."

Dana stared down into her lap. "She's very beautiful."

"Oh, Fayre's decorative. But it isn't for her looks that I keep her around, honey. You aren't that naive," he added meaningfully.

"No," she murmured, I'm not."

"You don't approve?" he laughed softly. "Men are creatures of strong appetites, little innocent, and mine were never lukewarm."

She felt her face going red and cleared her throat. "Uh...I like the music," she said quickly, listening to snatches of the tape. "Isn't it Scherezade?"

"It is," came the amused reply. "Frank, turn it up."

"Yes, sir," came the equally amused response from the front seat.

* * *

Adrian left Dana peering in store windows on the spacious mall while he strode purposefully into the jewelers. Her mind swept away by the gorgeous, ultra-chic outfits in the window displays, she was barely aware of time passing until he came up beside her.

"Ready? Or would you rather window shop some more?" he asked with a smile.

She shook her head. "I enjoy it, but I am a little hungry."

He studied her face. "If you like, we'll come back another day and I'll buy you one of those ensembles."

"Oh, no! No, thank you!" she said quickly, embarrassed. Did it look as if she wanted him to outfit her, had she given him the impression…!

"Stop it, for God's sake!" he said shortly. "My God, Dana, there isn't anyone who's less a golddigger than you… Don't you think I know you by now?"

"You don't know me at all."

"No?" A wisp of a smile touched his chiseled mouth as he stood there, looking down at her, oblivious to the interested glances of passing shoppers. "I know that you like to go barefoot on the carpet when you think no one's looking. You like books by Kahlil Gibran, and Debussy, and sunsets over Lake Lanier. You speak French, you don't approve of love affairs, you're twenty-three years old, and you love children. My God, Dana, what else do I need to know about you?"

She gaped at him, stunned by the scope of his knowledge. "You didn't add that I was a cheat, a liar, a loose woman…!" she cried, shaken.

His hand came up to stop the words as they formed on her lips. For a long time, his dark eyes stared straight down into hers, until her heart began to race and her knees threatened to melt under her.

"I know the truth now," he said gently, "I know how very innocent you are, little taffy cat. Do you know, Dana, your eyes are the exact shade of chestnuts when they first break out of the hull? And that your mouth…" His eyes caressed it with an intensity that burned her. "God, if we weren't surrounded by half of Atlanta, I'd kiss it now…!'' he whispered huskily.

She ducked her head, her cold nervous hands resting momentarily against his gray suitcoat while she got her balance back.

He laughed softly, taking one of her soft hands in his big one to squeeze it. ''Come on, little witch,'' he murmured deeply. ''I'm starving.''

She followed him into the cozy little creperie, with its wooden tables and benches and exquisite art prints on the walls, her hand still held tightly in his.

She tugged half-heartedly at the warm clasp, but he wouldn't let go.

''Adrian, what will people think?'' she asked anxiously.

A short, harsh chuckle burst from his mouth as he seated her. ''Probably,'' he said with unmistakable bitterness, ''that I'm taking my daughter to lunch.''

She met his cynical gaze squarely as he stood beside her, and the look on that dark face made her throw caution to the winds.

''I've never known a man I felt less daughterly toward,'' she said softly.

He drew a sharp breath. As he sat down, his face hardened to stone, his eyes became fierce and blackly burning as they met hers. "God, what a place to pick to tell me about it!" he whispered in a voice thick with feeling. "Damn you…!"

She flinched at the fury in his voice, puzzled by it, frightened by it. She averted her eyes to the waitress as a menu was handed to her. Adrian ordered coffee first, in a voice that was curt even for him. She didn't speak, giving him time to cool off, wondering vaguely what she'd done to create that terrible fury in him.

"What do you see that you like?" Adrian asked in a deep, taut voice.

"This chicken and broccoli crepe looks good," she replied, "and the one with two kinds of cheeses. And, oh, the strawberry crepe with cream…!"

The waitress came back with two steaming mugs of coffee and Adrian gave her the order and the menus. Then she was gone, and the full force of those stormy, angry eyes was on Dana's face again. Without a word, he took a small package from his pocket and placed it in front of her.

It was a jeweler's box, and she stared at it numbly, her lips parted on questions she couldn't ask.

"Will you open it?" he asked impatiently.

With trembling fingers she picked it up and lifted the lid. There, against the soft white satin, was a gemburst of emeralds and diamonds exquisitely mounted in a thin gold bracelet. "Oh...my goodness...for...not for me?" she stammered, her eyes stunned as they met his.

"Happy birthday, Dana," he said softly.

Tears filled her soft brown eyes, washing over the reddening rims, trickling down her flushed cheeks in a flood of emotion, her mouth trembling with the intensity of her feelings. He'd remembered her birthday!

Eight

It had been so long since anyone had wished her a happy birthday, or given her a present…

His big hand reached across the table and grasped hers in a warm, strong clasp, his fingers gently caressing. With his free hand, he reached in his pocket and handed her a handkerchief.

"Dry your eyes, Persephone," he said gently. "You'll water down that good coffee."

She nodded, wiping her face with the handkerchief with one hand while the other held on to Adrian's as if it were a lifeline.

"Thank you, Adrian, it's beautiful," she murmured with a watery smile. "It's the most beautiful present I've ever had. How did you know?"

"You told me when we were talking the other night," he said. His eyes probed hers. "Seventeen years between us now, Persephone. Too many."

He let her hand go and reached for his coffee. "I hope you're hungry," he said casually, as the waitress approached with plates of steaming crepes. Dana spent the rest of the lunch alternately eating and staring at the bracelet. But as she considered the expense it must have entailed, her conscience began to nag her.

In the car, she fiddled with the jeweler's box nervously. "Adrian?"

"What?" he asked curtly, his eyes on some distant point outside the window.

"I can't accept this."

His dark eyes jerked back to her face,

pinning her. "Why not? I hadn't planned on asking you to pay for it, little girl," he growled.

She flinched at his tone. "That's not what I meant," she said weakly. "It's just that it's so expensive…"

"How the hell do you know it isn't costume jewelry?" he demanded. His eyes studied her insolently. "What makes you think I'd consider you worth the real thing?"

She closed her eyes against the pain that those careless words had caused. For a little while, all the old angers had been put aside. But he was bringing them back with a vengeance.

With trembling fingers, she lifted the box and handed it to him, without looking up. "You'd better have it back," she said in a voice like shattered glass.

He took it from her and casually stuck it in his pocket. "I'll give it to Fayre," he said carelessly. "She likes trinkets."

She turned her attention to the landscape passing by the window, tears brimming over in her hurt eyes. It had started out to be such a nice birthday...

"Are you trying to drive me out of my mind?" he asked in a silky, cold voice. "Why the hell are you crying?"

She blinked back the tears, anger coming to her rescue. She threw a sparkling, furious glance in his general direction.

"I wouldn't give you the satisfaction of tears, *Mr.* Devereaux," she said icily. "You had me on my knees once, but don't ever expect to have me there again. I'll stick out these six months if I have to chew nails, I'll live for them to end!"

"That makes two of us," he growled under his breath.

The strained silence lasted all the way to the next stop on the tour—one of Adrian's sprawling manufacturing companies on the outskirts of the city. It was a hot day, and the haze of pollution enveloped the city like gauze. In the comfortable, air-conditioned Rolls, Dana had hardly noticed the heat. But she felt it with a vengeance as she walked beside Adrian toward the massive one-level factory through an arch with Devereaux Textiles engraved on it.

Adrian lit a cigarette as they walked, his first in her company that day, and blew out a cloud of gray smoke.

"We employ four hundred people here," he said, gesturing toward the brick exterior of the building. "We recently added a new air conditioning system to bring us up to par with the federal standards—it cuts down on the noise. Have you ever been inside a manufacturing plant?"

She shook her head. "I've always wondered how clothes were made, though."

"You'll get a good look at it in here." He held the glass door open for her and she felt the temperature dropping pleasantly as the air conditioning washed over her burning skin.

"That innovative production method…" she queried.

"Reporter to the sole of your shoes, aren't you?" he asked. Glittering malice was in his eyes as he looked down into hers.

She glared back at him. "It's kept me from going on welfare for a number of years," she replied coolly.

He turned away with a muttered curse. "I'll show it to you before we leave," he said curtly. "First we'll stop by Olsen's office—he's the plant manager."

Jack Olsen was tall and balding, very pleasant and obviously proud of his plant. Beside him was a slender, blond man with a quick smile and laughing blue eyes.

"This is Patrick Melbourne—Pat to most of us," Olsen said, introducing him. "He was a reporter before we enticed him into our personnel office with luxuries like real two-week vacations and an unlisted phone number."

Dana laughed as she hadn't laughed in years, the sound of it like silver bells, and Adrian glowered at it.

She took Pat Melbourne's hand with pleasure. "From one escapee to another," she told him, "congratulations!"

"Not you, too?" Pat asked with a grin,

looking her over with obvious appreciation. "The profession's improved in the five years since I left it."

"Only superficially," she told him. "The pay still isn't as good as what you get in industry, the hours are just as long, the phone rings off the hook all night and on weekends, and you still get yelled at for misspelled names on the society page—whether or not you're responsible. And I loved every minute of it, how about you?"

Sighing, he shrugged. "Same here, but I had expensive tastes—I liked three square meals a day and driving a car that wasn't ten years old. Now," he added with a malicious grin, "I drive a two year old car and eat two whole meals a day!"

She laughed again, delighted. "What paper did you work for?" she asked.

"One of the Miami papers," he said, and named it.

She gasped. "But that's the paper I'm with...was with," she corrected.

He leaned closer, lowering his voice secretively. "If I say the password, will you have dinner with me tonight?"

"What is the password?" she replied just as softly.

"Charlie wants it," he whispered.

She grinned. "What time shall I be ready?"

"Six sharp, and where do I pick you up?"

"At my home," Devereaux replied for her, his eyes narrowed and dangerous. "Meredith is my secretary. She's taking a…break…from reporting."

Pat nodded. "Let a story get to you?" he asked her quietly.

She nodded back. "It's better now."

"I understand."

"If you're through," Devereaux said in a voice like cold steel, "my time is limited. I'd like to get the tour over with."

"Of course, sir!" Olsen said quickly. "Whenever you're ready."

Recognizing the sharp look he got as a warning, Pat volunteered to stay behind and interview one of three job applicants in the waiting room.

"Kind of you to volunteer," Devereaux said pointedly. "That is your job, I presume, as head of personnel?"

One of Pat's eyebrows went up. "One of them, yes," he replied, and if he was intimidated, it didn't show.

Devereaux turned toward the door. "Let's go, Olsen."

"Yes, sir! Right this way..."

The first thing that impressed Dana was the size and spaciousness of the building. The tile floors were strangely clean for the number of employees. Most of them, she noticed, were women. They sat at row upon row of sewing machines, and the noise was ear-splitting. Occasionally, men would move among the women with what looked like ragged bundles of colorful cloth. Other men moved through the unit with large buggies of cloth, or passed down the aisle on their way to the canteen for coffee or snacks.

"This is the shirt line," Olsen was explaining, gesturing toward the first of the large sections. "Each woman performs a particular function in the manufacture of a shirt—one may sew sides seams while another puts on sleeves, and so forth. The women you see standing up, moving around the machines, are called floor ladies. They're the supervisors.''

''How about those men there?'' Dana asked, nodding toward two young men carrying the bundles.

Olsen chuckled. ''They're called, believe it or not, bundle boys. If a girl does it, she's called a bundle girl. They carry pieces of a garment to be sewn to the women who do that particular section of the shirt.''

Dana watched, fascinated at the speed of the women as they ran the material out with deft, quick hands. Olsen went on to explain that they had to meet a deadline and that their pay depended on how fast they could sew.

They were in the cutting room, where tables ran the length of the building and men were busily at work cutting out huge layers of cloth with what looked like jigsaws, when one of the office girls came quickly toward them.

"I'm sorry to interrupt," she apologized, "but there's an urgent message for Mr. Devereaux. Mr. Hall called from your office and said that a man named Winston was waiting to see you, sir."

"Winston!" Adrian sighed heavily. "That's right. Let's go, Dana, I'll bring you back another day to finish the tour. Olsen, thanks anyway."

"My pleasure, sir. If Miss Meredith would like to stay..." he offered.

"She comes with me," Devereaux said in a firm voice, with a hard glance at Dana.

"Back down into the catacombs again, boss?" she asked in a sweet tone.

"You've got it, Persephone," he murmured darkly.

He managed to get her outside and into the car without Pat seeing her, and she seethed at his possessive attitude.

"You don't own me," she said quietly, on the way back to the manor. "I have a right to go out with a man if I want to."

"Man?" he scoffed. "He couldn't be over twenty-six."

She glanced at the hard expression on

his face. "At least he isn't over the hill, like some people I could name!"

He turned slowly in the seat, and met her eyes levelly. His were dark and quiet and threatening.

"Little girl," he said in a voice that chilled, "someday I'm going to make a point of showing you just how 'over the hill' I happen to be. And it'll be an experience you won't forget, I promise you."

She jerked her gaze away, blushing faintly. "Thank you for my lunch, anyway," she said politely.

There was a deep, resigned sigh from the other side of the car. "Dana, this isn't how I planned your birthday to turn out," he said, almost regretfully.

"What did you have in mind, sir?" she asked tightly. "Party hats and balloons and noisemakers, and a little cake with my name on it?"

"Damn you," he whispered deeply, and his hand shot out, catching her wrist to jerk her across his lap and into his big, merciless arms.

She found her head thrust against his

shoulder, his eyes blazing down into hers, his warm breath whipping across her mouth.

His big hand found her cheek, his fingers caressing, his eyes searching hers in a silence that seemed to last forever, the traffic noises drowned out, time suspended around them.

"This is what I had in mind," he whispered softly, bending his head. His mouth whispered against hers as the words had brushed her ears, softly, sensuously, seductively. "Don't fight me this time... little taffy kitten, don't fight..."

His lips moved deeper and deeper against hers, the kiss hardening, his arms crushing, the need in him like a fever burning her, consuming her.

Instinctively, frightened of the sensations he was arousing, she started to push against his broad chest, but he caught her soft hand and drew it up against his mouth, kissing the palm.

"There's nothing to be afraid of," he murmured gruffly, his eyes holding hers. "I know you're a babe in the woods, despite what I've said. I'll never hurt you. Never.''

Her lips trembled. "But, you said..."

His hand brushed the tumbled hair away from her face. "Forget what I said. Dana, I'm just a man," he whispered, "imperfect and hot-tempered, fond of having everything my own way. But I'm not a monster. God, why can't you trust me? Even now, in my arms, your body trembles as if I've whipped you. Why do I frighten you so?''

She lowered her eyes to his tie. "You know too much," she murmured breathlessly.

"Not enough," he mused, tightening his hold on her slender body. "Those seventeen years—they bother you like hell, don't they?" he asked bitterly.

Shocked, she looked up into his hard eyes. "I don't think I've ever given it a thought," she murmured, absently telling the truth.

His eyes sketched her face slowly. "You're just a baby, aren't you?" he whispered softly. "Just a silky little girl. I think I know how Pluto must have felt.''

Involuntarily, her fingers went up to touch his broad, chiseled mouth, tracing its outline. "I'm sorry about the bracelet," she said gently. "But I thought it must be horribly expensive, and I had nothing to give you in return..."

"Little Miss Independence," he breathed, shaking his head. "Nothing to give me? How about a kiss, Meredith? Just one, freely given and we'll call it quits."

She considered it for several seconds and then, with a tiny sigh that almost betrayed the hunger she was feeling, she reached up and put her mouth to his. She felt him stiffen at the caress, felt the awesome muscles tighten in his big arms and his massive chest.

That tensing puzzled her and she drew back abruptly, looking into eyes that frightened her. His face was like carved stone, his eyes blistering, glittering, his jaw clenched, his breath coming in heavy sighs.

They pulled up in front of the house, and he took the jeweler's box from his pocket, tossing it idly into her lap.

"T...thank you," she managed.

"What for?" he demanded. "It's paid for," he added coldly.

She turned away, hurt, and reached for the door handle.

"Are you still planning to go out with that ex-news hound tonight?" he asked harshly.

She froze. "I did accept," she reminded him.

"I want you back in the house by midnight," he told her. "I'm not going to have my secretary walking around in a yawning stupor because of late nights. Is that clear?"

"Yes, sir," she said through her teeth. "It's clear."

She got out of the car and marched into the house, oblivious to the heat, the sound of the Rolls purring down the driveway—and the pair of dark eyes that watched her until she was out of sight.

Defiantly, she wore a new, exotic dress for the date, a swirling confection of aqua chiffon that had a neckline that just escaped immodesty. She put her hair up into a loose topknot, leaving tiny curls around her face, and loaded her throat and wrists with perfume. She paid more attention than usual to cosmetics as well, and a stranger stared back at her from the mirror in her room.

"Wow," Lillian said when she came downstairs, "who are you out to impress?"

"A comrade at arms," she replied tightly. "An ex-reporter who makes me laugh, which is a nice change for me."

"Hmm," Lillian said. "A new fella?"

"One of Mr. Devereaux's employees, if we have to get technical about it," came the reply. "And a very nice man."

"That reminds me," Lillian said, "the Mister called while you were in the tub to say he wouldn't be in until late. He said to remind you about midnight—that make any sense?" she added with a frown.

Dana flushed. "Oh, yes, it makes sense," she replied, thinking she'd come home when she was bloody well ready, and if he didn't like it, he could lump it!

Lillian eyed her closely. "I don't suppose you'd know why he was in such a bad mood? I asked him if he was taking the dragon out, and he said, 'hell, yes, he was,' and that it was all your fault."

She felt an empty sensation in the pit of her stomach. Surely, he hadn't planned to take her out to supper...?

The doorbell rang, cutting into the conversation, and Pat Melbourne was standing outside the door in a stylish rust-colored jacket with matching shirt and dark slacks, and a warm smile.

He gave her a long wolf-whistle when he finished his thorough scrutiny. "Lovely lady, I feel inadequate to escort a princess."

She frowned thoughtfully. "Doesn't that have something to do with lily ponds and magic spells?"

"And your friendly neighborhood frog," he added with a grin. "Shall we proceed? My pumpkin awaits without."

"Wrong fairly tale," she reminded him. "And, personally, I prefer unicorns to pumpkins."

"I'll remember."

Unicorns. Adrian. She sighed as she got into the comfortable coupe with Pat. Everything seemed to remind her of the dark prince, even the night. Her mind drifted back to that walk in the garden when the white roses were all around them—to the lake and the feel of his big arms swallowing her on the dance floor. She felt her heart leap. And then, there was today, and the bracelet. She'd worn it against all her misgivings, and she touched it now, ran her fingers over that cold green fire that burned no less than the feeling in her heart for the man who'd given it to her. It matched my dress, she told herself, and turned her attention quickly to Pat.

"How did you get into reporting in the first place?" she asked him.

He laughed softly. "I was kidnapped by a wandering tribe of itinerant poets who sold me to an editor," he told her. "You have to admit it sounds more romantic than saying I went through four years of journalism school and walked right into a job as a police reporter."

"I was general assignments," she replied. "I wasn't sure I could handle the police beat."

"It can get rough," he recalled. "I covered a murder once and the suspect's brother caught me in a dark alley one night and beat me up. He was a professional fighter it turned out, and the publicity hadn't helped him any more than it had helped his brother."

"Ouch," she murmured. "Did it do any lasting damage?"

"Sure did," he admitted with a grin. "It destroyed my faith in humanity."

She laughed. "Were you at it long enough to get hardboiled?"

"Anybody who stays in it for more than three years full-time gets hardboiled," he said quietly. "You can't keep caring with an amateur's intensity—it'll tear your guts out. You found that out, didn't you?"

She nodded. They were stopped at a traffic light, with the brilliant street lights and business signs making visual fireworks all around them in the darkness. They highlighted the soft lines of her face.

"I covered a flood," she said quickly. "Most of the victims were children."

"I understand," he replied. "That kind of thing you don't ever get hardened to. Maybe it's a good sign. What good is a reporter who can't feel?"

"Not much. But things get to me more than they used to."

"Did you talk about it to someone?" he asked, pulling the car forward as the light changed.

"Yes." "Oh, yes," she could have told him, "I rambled on and cried for an eternity in my boss' arms in the middle of the night." But that might have sounded just a bit unconventional, so she kept it to herself.

"Still want to go back to it?" he persisted.

She took a deep breath. "I don't know. That's honest. Sometimes I feel as if I don't even exist. I'm just a pad and a pen and a camera. Do you know, I get invited to places I couldn't even get into if I weren't a reporter?!"

He nodded. "It goes with the job.

And,'' he added humorously, "you catch the down for everything that ever goes wrong—classified ads with missing phone numbers, society news with misspelled names—and never mind that you don't have anything to do with those departments. You work for the paper, so it's your fault.''

"Gosh, you really do miss it, don't you?'' Dana teased.

He drew a deep breath. "Yeah. I really do miss it. But I don't plan to stay single all my life, and I had to make a move or end up begging jobs as a copywriter just to keep my hand in. It gets in your blood.''

"I know. Part of me wants to go back.'' She lowered her eyes. "Part of me wants to forget that I ever knew how to type.''

"The advantage of being a personnel chief for a plant,'' Pat told her, "is that if a bank gets robbed at two a.m., nobody calls you up to tell you about it.''

She smiled. "How lovely!''

"Your boss didn't want you to come out with me tonight,'' he said as he pulled the car into the parking lot of a seafood chain restaurant and cut off the engine. "Does he have a claim on you?"

She drew a long breath. "Three years ago I was working for a magazine and I put on a disguise and went to work for Adrian Devereaux as a secretary to get the inside story of his wife's death. To make a long story short, a terrible error was made that the proofreader didn't catch, and it ruined him. He lost everything. It's taken him those years in-between to climb back up to the top, and somebody has to pay for what happened. Since I wrote the story...well, you get the general idea." She glanced at him, at his suddenly set features. "I think I might have preferred your professional fighter in a dark alley."

"You could walk out," he said shortly.

"He could have me brought back." She fingered the beautiful bracelet. "Besides," she added softly, "it isn't as bad as I expected it to be. In many ways, he's a very lonely man."

He muttered something noncommittal and came around to open the door. "I hope you like seafood," he said. "I didn't even ask…"

"Oh, I like seafood very much. I once did a story," she recalled, "about a retired seaman who did woodcarvings."

"Tell me about it."

And she did. They traded memories, and stories, all evening. Pat was easy to be with, easy to talk to. She enjoyed it, and sensed that he did too. It was good to just sit and talk shop, to talk about writing and reporting with someone who could say more than, "oh, how nice," and change the subject.

"Let's do this again," Pat said as he let her out at the front door just after one o'clock in the morning.

"All right," she agreed with a smile.

"Saturday? We'll drive up into the mountains, and I'll show you a small town that'll make you think you're in Germany."

"Really?" she teased. "Well, I'll hunt up my *dirndl*!"

"Eight o'clock too early for you?" he asked.

She shook her head. "I'm am early bird. See you then."

"It's a date. Goodnight."

She waved to him and went up the steps lazily. She was still recalling bits and pieces of conversation when she got inside, only to come face to face with sudden reality.

Adrian stood at the foot of the steps, still fully dressed except for his jacket and tie, looking like a stormy day.

"I said midnight," he told her quietly.

"I'm simply years past my sixteenth birthday," she said in a juvenile voice, raising her face impudently. "Unless you want to adopt me and put me back in patent leather shoes and ruffles, you'd do better to live your own life and let me manage mine. I've been doing it without your help for a long time."

His eyes narrowed, glittering and angry. "You belong to me for six months, Persephone," he reminded her, "and for those six months if I yell jump, you ask 'how high?' Is that clear?"

She stood her ground. "I work for you.

I don't belong to you!'' she threw back at him.

"Don't you, honey?'' His eyes centered on the lovely bracelet she'd forgotten to put in her purse, watching the light scatter it into green glints of fire against her slender wrist. "You might as well be wearing a brand. Did you tell Melbourne where it came from?''

"He didn't **have** the bad manners to ask,'' she returned.

"Why are you wearing it at all?'' he demanded in a tone that held the suggestion of a threat.

She swallowed nervously. ''It...matches my dress,'' she said in a thin voice.

He shouldered away from the banister he'd been leaning against and came toward her lazily. He stopped just in front of her and touched a big, gentle hand to the bun on top of her head.

"Did you have fun?'' he asked carelessly.

"We...we went to a seafood restaurant and had fried oysters,'' she replied, drowning in the scent of his masculine aftershave lotion, the nearness of his big, warm body.

"And talked shop?" he persisted gently.

"Well, yes," she said weakly. Her eyes traced the open collar of his shirt. "We...we talked about stories we'd covered and I told him about the...the flood...."

"You told me about it, too, remember?" he asked in a slow, seductive tone. "In my arms at two in the morning."

"I don't have nightmares anymore," she murmured evasively.

"I frightened you out of your wits," he recalled gently. "I thought you were worldly, and sophisticated, and found to my horror..."

"Please, I'm very...tired," she whispered quickly.

His fingers traced the flush in her cheek. "Do I torment you, little girl?" he mused deeply. "It works both ways, you know."

She lifted her curious eyes to his. He caught the wrist that was adorned by the emerald bracelet and put it to his lips in a gesture that was strangely exciting.

"Happy birthday, Persephone," he murmured. "You look like an angel and I feel like the devil, and I really think you'd better get up those stairs while I remind myself how immoral it would be to seduce a little taffy kitten seventeen years my junior."

The look in his eyes made her head for the stairs. "I thought that required a little cooperation," she said over her shoulder with forced bravado.

"Dana."

She turned and met his eyes, saw the confidence, the patience in them.

"After the first thirty seconds," he said very quietly, "you wouldn't be fighting me."

She swallowed down the fear. "I call that conceit."

He smiled, a sensuous smile that made her pulse race. "Little girl, if you think I've gone through my entire routine with you, you're even less sophisticated than I gave you credit for." The smile deepened.

"I think, very soon, I'm going to fill in some of the gaps in your education."

"Oh, no, you're not!" she returned.

His eyes went up and down her slender figure, lingering on the deep cut of the bodice. "A challenge like that can be a subtle invitation, did you know?"

"No, but I'll bet the dragon does," she said without thinking.

Both dark brows went up together and knitted. "The dragon?"

In too deep to back out, she lifted her face proudly. "Miss Braunns," she said carelessly.

A tiny smile curved his mouth. "Jealous, honey?" he asked insolently.

She flushed angrily. "I don't envy her in your bed, if that's what you mean!" she flashed.

"How would you know, little cat," he asked in a low, soft tone, "since you've yet to share my bed in that respect? Not forgetting," he added wickedly, "that you've slept in my arms."

"That was...that was entirely... innocent!" she faltered.

"On your part," he corrected. He paused to light a cigarette. "I learned the tortures of the damned before I finally got to sleep," he said quietly.

She gaped at him, her eyes curious as they met the deep hunger in his.

"If you don't stop looking at me like that..." he warned in a tight, husky voice.

The hint was enough. She turned and ran up the stairs.

Nine

It wasn't until she and Pat were pulling into the small remodeled Alpine village of Helen that Dana began to wonder why Adrian had been waiting for her the night before.

As they wandered through the Bavarian-style shops and merged with the crush of tourists, it played on her mind. Could it be possible that he was jealous of her? For just an instant, she was on top of the world—until she remembered that he'd been out with Fayre. Probably he'd only just got in himself and was on his way upstairs when he heard her arrive. Her heart fell.

"Hey, why the long face?" Pat teased, and pulled her arm through his as they walked back toward the car. "There's a short order place across the street. Let's get a few hot dogs and some fries and go picnic on the Chattahoochee. Would you like that?"

Her face lit up. "Oh, yes! Could we go to that little roadside park in Robertstown?" she asked.

"I thought I was showing you someplace new," he teased.

She shook her head with a smile. "I used to work for a small weekly a few miles away. I know this part of the state like the back of my hand."

"We live and learn," Pat said with a wry shake of his head.

It was like finding a tiny spot of heaven, the little roadside park with its towering oaks leaning out over the wide, bubbling river and its stone tables and benches.

Dana barely took time to eat before she clambered down the bank, holding on to the exposed roots of a huge sycamore, and walked barefooted into the cold water.

"Careful you don't fall in," Pat called to her from the safety of the bank.

"I'm a river rat," she called back. "I've been all the way down to Helen in this river in an inner tube, and I've got the scars to prove it."

"Crazy woman," Pat sighed. "Typical reporter. Why do we take risks like that, hmm?"

She gazed at the fast running water as it slipped over the huge boulders made smooth by years of watery friction, at the low hanging branches, with their emerald green leaves, at the shady, watery peace of the river.

"Pat, would life really be worth living without a little danger?" she asked quietly.

He shrugged. "I'm not sure."

She closed her eyes and listened to the water as it whispered noisily in its banks, wondering vaguely at the peace it gave her. The sound of running water once had fostered nightmares. Now, when she thought about it, all she seemed to remember was a pair of hard arms holding her, rocking her, and the sound of a deep voice murmuring against her hair. She sighed with a tiny smile.

"I hate to break up what looks like a lifelong love affair," Pat called, "but it's getting late, and it is a two hour drive back."

She waded back to shore and pulled herself up on the bank. Her face was alight with pleasure as she smiled up at Pat.

"Thank you for today," she told him. "It's been delicious."

He chuckled. "I couldn't have put it better myself. I enjoyed it too, and I wish we could stay longer. But sometimes the job goes home with me, and this is one of those weekends. Thanks," he added darkly, "to our mutual boss."

"I don't understand," she said, following him to the car.

"Call it homework," he said with a wry grin.

She grimaced. "Spite would be a better adjective."

"You told me he didn't have any claim on you," he said as he cranked the car and pulled out into traffic.

"We had an argument about the time I was supposed to get in last night," she replied quietly. "One of many small disagreements that keep cropping up. It's me he's really after, not you, even though it may seem like it."

"In that case," Pat grinned, "maybe you could get him to give *you* overtime work instead of me."

"Patrick my friend, for you I'll try," she laughed.

But she didn't. Because for the next few days, Adrian Devereaux was as remote and cold as one of the outer planets. He barely spoke to her except on business, and each time Patrick called for her at night to take her out, he shut himself up in his den and didn't even speak to the young man. It came as something of a shock when he came home early Friday afternoon and told her to start packing.

"We're going to the lake for the weekend," he said shortly.

"We?" she echoed.

"You and Lillian and I," he growled, "who the hell did you think I meant?"

She flinched at the tone. "I thought...I mean, Miss Braunns called this morning and said that you were taking her to the cabin...."

"Did she?" he asked darkly.

"Yes." What an inadequate word, she thought, to describe what Fayre had really said—the venom in her voice as she told Dana how "affectionate" Adrian had been lately, and how she was looking forward to an uninterrupted weekend with him, and how Dana had damned sure better guarantee that they weren't disturbed. But she didn't tell him that. She only said, "Yes."

"Do you swim?" he asked suddenly.

"No, sir," she replied without thinking.

He turned on her, his eyes black, his face heavily lined and tired. "How many times do I have to tell you not to call me sir?"

She swallowed nervously. "I'm sorry,"

she met his threatening gaze levelly. "Must I go?" she added softly. "I had planned…"

"He's in Chicago," he told her with narrowed eyes.

Both eyebrows went up. "Pat? But we were going…"

"Were is right. You're coming to the lake with me. You've got exactly thirty minutes to pack." He turned back to his desk, thumbing through papers.

She opened her mouth to argue, but thought better of it. She sighed as she went out the door. Talk about homework, she thought miserably, it looked like this was going to be a honey of a working weekend. He'd probably saved up every bit of correspondence for her. With a grimace she went to her room to pack.

Leaving Frank behind, Adrian drove the Mercedes, with Dana in front and Lillian comfortably relaxed in the back seat. They reached Gainesville in no time, and he stopped at a big chain supermarket.

"Sir," Lillian protested, "the freezer's full, and the cabinet's stocked…"

He grinned as he got out of the small car. "Not with what I want. Come on!"

The years had fallen away. He seemed younger, more relaxed—almost carefree. And the charm he was turning full force on Dana was devastating.

He pushed the grocery cart himself. "Lillian," he told the older woman, "get me some lettuce and tomatoes and onions from the produce counter."

She frowned. "You going to make a salad?" she asked.

"I'm going to make a scene if you don't get going," he threatened, not even breaking stride as he headed for the dairy counter.

Lillian went, shaking her head, and Dana followed her boss. He was picking up some flat meal cakes.

"Get me a carton of sour cream," he told her, nodding toward the nearby section of yogurt and creams.

With a puzzled glance, she picked up a large one and brought it back, handing it to him.

"Now," he said. "Ground beef."

"Think we can get it without mortgaging one of your cars?" Dana asked cheekily.

He looked down at her with quiet amusement in his eyes. "For that," he said, "you can help me cook supper. We're giving Lillian the night off in the kitchen. What do you want for dessert?"

She caught her breath, aglow at the possibilities. "How about," she murmured thoughtfully, "some of those frozen eclairs? Do you like chocolate?"

"Go get it," he told her, "and anything else that you want."

She darted off to the frozen goods section, her mind whirling with the possibilities. The grocery store had always been someplace to go with a very tight list of necessities. To be able to choose a dessert without looking at the price and sacrificing something else for it was new and exciting.

She grabbed up the eclairs and forced herself not to look at the price tag. He was waiting for her at the meat counter.

"Is that all you wanted?" he asked incredulously.

She shrugged with a tiny smile. "I don't have very expensive tastes," she told him.

He met her eyes with a strange tenderness. "No, honey, you don't. It makes a man want to spoil the hell out of you."

She turned red as a beet, and was grateful for Lillian's sudden reappearance with the vegetables. "Here you are, Mr. Devereaux, but what are you going to do with them?"

"Dana and I are going to make tacos," he told her, "and you're going to sit down and put your feet up."

The older woman stood there looking as if she'd won the Irish Sweepstakes, her eyes wider than saucers. Tears began to mist in them, and she turned away quickly.

"Cut it out," Adrian said darkly. "You'll make me blush."

Lillian managed a short laugh. "That'll be the day. Here, you'll need some cheese, won't you? I'll get it."

Dana looked up at him with everything

she felt in her soft brown eyes. "You're a nice man," she told him.

He smiled. "It grates, little one. It grates."

Back at the cabin, Dana shredded lettuce and cheese while Adrian stood over the stove where the ground beef was sizzling away. Lillian, banished from the spacious kitchen overlooking the lake, was curled up on the living room sofa with a magazine.

"I hope you don't mind if the cheese is pink," she remarked idly.

"What?" he asked, half turning toward her with a question in his eyes. In the red sports shirt and white slacks, he was a devastating study in masculine beauty, his darkness complimented by the clothes he was wearing.

"Pink cheese," she repeated, holding a nipped finger to her lips. "I never grate anything at home because I'm so clumsy—I get more of me in what I'm grating than the stuff I'm preparing."

"Well, it isn't every day that the cook

gives her life's blood to her work," he teased gently.

She smiled back at him, and the room seemed to disappear around them.

The smell of burning beef finally caught his attention, and with a muffled curse, he turned back to the stove. "Damn it, woman, don't distract me like that," he growled softly. "I don't like my beef black and crunchy."

"I don't see why not," she laughed, delighted by the change in him, "it's the latest thing."

"Shred the damned lettuce and shut up."

"Yes, sir."

"And don't call me sir!"

"No, sir."

"Dana...!" he growled, making a threat out of her name.

She grinned down at the cheese as she drew it against the grater. He could be so much fun to be with. He made a simple adventure of cooking a meal. She sighed wistfully. If only it was her instead of Fayre that stirred that possessive nature of his. But it wasn't. And even if it had been, physical hungers didn't make up for the luxurious wonder that was love. That was what she wanted from Adrian, and he'd already admitted that when he married he hadn't known what it was.

Supper was delicious. They ate tacos and nibbled on pieces of tomato and cheese until Lillian threatened to burst with her next bite. She ignored the eclairs, shaking her head while Dana and Adrian finished the last one between them.

"Well, I'll clean up..." Lillian began, rising.

"I said you were having the night off," Adrian told her. "Dana and I will wash up."

Lillian smiled, shaking her head. "If you're sure. I did have my heart set on a movie in my room—they're showing a re-run of that comedy about gunfighters..."

"Go to it," Adrian grinned at her. "Come on, Dana, let's get it done."

Lillian was gone, and Dana started stacking the plates while Adrian ran water in the sink and searched for washrags and drying cloths.

"I used to do this with Daddy years ago," Dana recalled with a smile, as she reached past Adrian to set her dishes in the warm, soapy water.

His hands made contact with hers under the surface of the water. His eyes caught hers and held them. "Are you trying to tell me something?" he asked softly.

She couldn't look away. She couldn't answer him. Those dark, warm eyes were making chills up and down her spine, the closeness of that big, warm body made her hungry.

"Oh, Adrian," she breathed unsteadily, yielding to a sweetness that made her face glow in the soft kitchen light.

He drew her hands out of the sink and lifted them up around his neck, oblivious to their wetness, to the suds that reached to her tanned forearms.

"I'm wet..." she whispered shakily as his own arms went around her slender body, coaxing it against the hard warmth of his own.

"I don't care," he whispered deeply. "I want to kiss you. Close your eyes, little girl. I'll make it good for both of us…"

Trembling, burning, she let her heavy eyelids fall. She felt his mouth touch hers, whisper across it, and then, suddenly, burrow into it with a hunger that shook her heart. His big arms contracted like sunburned rawhide around her, hurting in their own hunger, bruising her. And for the first time, she held on to him, kissing him back with a fervor she'd never felt. And it was like dying, drifting, with the world falling out from under her feet, and she loved him…loved him!

He drew back, and she felt the tremor in his hard arms as he looked down at her with a tenderness in his face she wondered at.

"Not here," he whispered huskily. "Come on."

He caught her hand and strode out the back door, down the steps toward the car, towing her along behind him.

He opened the door of the Mercedes and put her inside, sliding in beside her.

''Where…where are we going?'' she asked, mindless, breathless with the effects of his ardor.

He reached out and drew her back into his arms, lifting her across his chest to lie with her head pillowed on his shoulder. ''We're not going anywhere,'' he murmured quietly. ''I wanted to be alone with you, and this was the only readily available spot. Don't talk, honey. Don't talk. Just feel, Dana…''

His mouth found hers again, tasting it, cherishing it with a lazy thoroughness that was vaguely reassuring. She reached trembling fingers up to caress his warm, hard jaw, the cool black silky hair at his temples, at the back of his head.

''Here,'' he whispered, his teeth nipping gently at her lower lip as he caught her hand and placed it on his broad chest.

She let her palm go flat against him, loving the strength and warmth under her cool fingers as she savored the tender crush of his mouth.

''Well?'' he murmured.

''What?'' she asked against his lips.

He drew back, his eyes puzzled, his heavy brows drawn together in a frown. His hand covered hers where it lay still against his chest. "Dana, haven't you ever touched a man... My God, child, I never realized just how unworldly you are until this minute," he breathed softly.

He flicked open the buttons of his shirt and moved her hand into the thick hair over the warm muscles.

Her hand stiffened unsurely and she felt rather than saw the patient smile on his face as he bent down toward her. "You touched me that night we were dancing in the cabin," he reminded her softly.

"I...I know, but it was different somehow," she breathed. "Adrian, you must know that you could...that I couldn't stop you..." She faltered over the words.

His lips brushed her hot cheek. "I know it very well, Persephone," he murmured quietly. "Why do you think I brought you out here instead of taking you into the den and locking the door?"

She let her head slide back on his hard arm so that she could look up into his eyes, quiet eyes in the dim light that sliced across the front seat from the house windows.

He let the back of his fingers run down her cheek, against her soft throat, into the opening of her low necked blouse, feeling her tremble under the slow caress.

"Do you let Pat Melbourne touch you like this?" he asked suddenly, the very quietness of his deep voice a threat in itself.

Under the spell of his lips, his deft, warm hands, it took a minute for the words to penetrate her swaying mind.

"Pat? He's my friend," she whispered. "He doesn't touch me at all."

"Doesn't he?" His eyes narrowed to slits. "You've been out with him every night for a week, and you expect me to believe that it's been platonic every minute?"

She tugged out of his arms, and sat up, gaping at him. "Yes, I expect you to believe it, because it's the truth!" she threw at him.

"Is it, really?" he gazed at her with

contempt in every line of his face. "God, you're easy," he said silkily. "All it took was one kiss, and you'd have followed me straight into my bedroom, wouldn't you, Meredith?"

She felt her face go white. He could think that...when she loved him enough to follow him straight into hell, and he couldn't see it.

Her eyes closed on a humiliation she couldn't bear him seeing. "I'll go back and finish the dishes," she said in a strained voice, reaching for the door handle.

"Do that." He reached in his pocket for keys. "I'm going back to the house. Fayre's waiting for me."

Ten

The cold words haunted her all through the long night. "Fayre's waiting for me." She wanted to find a hole and crawl into it. How could he, how could he?! The only good thing that had come out of that cruel night was that Lillian hadn't come out and seen the whiteness of her face, the tears trickling freely down her cheeks as she cried like a young girl.

Was it some form of vengeance, she wondered, and cursed her own stupidity for letting him see how much she wanted his kisses. That had amused him. And gave him the impression that she was an easy mark. At least he hadn't realized that she was in love with him. His blindness had been her salvation.

When morning came, her eyes were bloodshot and her face showed the effects of three hours' sleep. She used more makeup than she ever had to camouflage it, wondering all the while if Adrian had come back in the night, or if he planned to come back at all.

After breakfast she had the answer. Frank came with the car to take her and Lillian, who was wearing a puzzled frown, back to Atlanta.

They walked in the front door to find Fayre coming jauntily down the stairs with an overnight case in her hand. Dana felt something die inside her, and clutched her pride to her like a shield. She met Fayre's smiling face with a schooled indifference that made lights flash in the little blonde's pale eyes.

"Well, good morning," she cooed. "Did you have a good time at the lake?"

"An interesting one, anyway," Dana said coolly.

"That's nice. Well, I must be off. I have to…catch up on my sleep," she said with a secretive smile and simulated self-consciousness. "Goodbye. Tell Adrian I'll call him later."

Adrian! Dana managed a tight smile. "Of course."

Fayre went out the front door with a triumphant little laugh.

"Tramp!" Lillian whispered harshly, staring at the closed door. "What in this world has gotten into the Mister?!"

"Lillian!" came a roar from upstairs. "Get up here!"

Lillian's eyes narrowed. "He'll wish I hadn't," she promised, her lips set and her eyes flashing as she mounted the staircase.

Dana set her case under the hall table and went straight into the study. She sat down at the desk and got out the correspondence left over from Thursday. In minutes, her fingers were busy on the keys of the typewriter.

Lillian stuck her head in the door on the way upstairs with a tray of steaming coffee.

"If it's any consolation," she grinned, "he's got a head the size of all outdoors, and I think he hates himself. He must have really tied one on last night."

That was strange, she thought, what was there to make him drink? Or maybe, she sighed, Fayre had given him a reason.

By late afternoon, Adrian was back on his feet and in a darkly dangerous mood.

"Have you got an evening gown?" he asked Dana, pausing beside her desk as he picked up the telephone.

"Yes," she said shortly.

"Go put it on. There's a cocktail party at the Jamesons' tonight and we're going to discuss opening an outlet store. I'll need you there to take notes."

"Wouldn't a tape recorder do?" she asked coldly.

He gazed down at her with narrowed eyes. "I feel like hell," he said quietly.

"Keep it up, and I can guarantee you'll feel the same way when I'm through with you."

She clammed up. With a heavy sigh, she left the typewriter and went upstairs to change clothes. It was going to be a perfectly horrible evening. She dreaded it even as she put on the clinging brandy colored knit dress and started working on her makeup.

She almost put her hair into a bun because she knew he hated it, but his mood was unpredictable, and she had visions of him ripping hairpins out in front of a startled group of partygoers. She left it long and loose and went downstairs with all the gaiety of a condemned woman walking to the gallows.

He came out of the den, checking his cuffs, devastatingly handsome in his black evening clothes, his black hair still damp from a shower. He smelled of expensive cologne, and just the sight of the man was enough to quicken her pulse.

His dark eyes swept up and down her body with a slow, thorough boldness that made her burn. "If you'd been wearing that last night..." He left it unsaid, but she anticipated the words and blushed.

"Come on, Dana, we don't want to be late," he said carelessly, holding the door open for her.

"No, sir," she said deliberately.

And this time, he didn't argue.

The Jamesons had a large brick home on a wooded lot that was every bit as big as Adrian's. Dana's first impression inside the house was of crystal and light. Even the guests seemed to glitter.

"Don't let it intimidate you," Adrian told her. "The Jamesons are just people. Very nice people."

She only nodded, feeling lost and alone and vaguely afraid. Crowds bothered her. They always had.

"Reporters are supposed to love crowds and strangers and bright lights," Adrian reminded her gently. He reached down for her hand and felt it tremble in his firm, warm grasp, curling up in a token protest. "Stay close to me, little taffy kitten," he murmured, softly, "and I'll protect you."

"Who'll protect me from you?" she grumbled unsteadily.

His fingers moved on hers gently, seductively, entwining with hers against all her better judgment as she let him force her taut hand open. "Trust me."

"I can't," she whispered unsteadily. "I can't ever trust you again."

"Was it seeing Fayre come down those stairs this morning?" he asked solemnly.

"I don't particularly care where Miss Braunns sleeps," she told him with a calm indifference that was quite convincing.

His jaw set menacingly. "No more than you care where you sleep?"

She didn't have to answer him. The Jamesons appeared suddenly, drawing the two of them into the room with laughter and introductions that made Dana's mind whirl. They were, as Adrian had said, nice people. But they were also strangers, and they made her nervous.

Adrian grasped her hand tightly in his and kept her close by his side until they had made the rounds of the guests.

Then he drew her with him out to the

patio, where several couples had a massive stereo set up and were dancing to soft music under the torch lamps and shards of moonlight filtering through the trees.

"I...thought you came here to talk business," Dana protested as he took her into his big arms and began to dance.

"I'm going to get you calmed down first," he replied gently. "Relax, honey. Just relax, they're people like the rest of us, and they're probably every bit as nervous as you are."

"How did you know I was nervous?" she asked him.

He only smiled. "I know you very well, Miss Meredith," he replied quietly.

"You think you do," she countered, letting her body relax just a little in the close, comforting circle of his hard arms.

His big hand ran down her smooth bare back to the zipper, then down still lower to her waist over the smooth material, slow and gentle and caressing.

"This is too inhibiting," he murmured at her temple.

She felt her cheeks burn. "Will you

please remember that my name is Dana, not Fayre?'' she asked icily.

A soft, deep chuckle passed his lips. ''Were you jealous, little cat?'' he asked.

''Of you? You're my boss, not my...'' she paused over the word.

''...lover?'' he supplied, and drew back enough to look down into her soft brown eyes. ''No, I'm not, but I'd like to be.''

She jerked her gaze down to his dark jacket. ''I wouldn't like it,'' she denied huskily.

''Then why did you follow me out to the Mercedes?'' he taunted. ''For all you know, I might have been taking you to a motel room.''

''You wouldn't do that.''

He caught her eyes. ''You're learning,'' he said gently.

She glared up at him, all the anguish coming back. ''I'm not easy!'' she threw at him.

''Not with other men, no,'' he said, and his hand tightened around hers. ''But you are with me, and I want to know why.''

''It's a fixation,'' she lied glibly. ''I've

always been crazy about Anthony Quinn, and you remind me of him in a physical sense.''

He laughed softly down at her, his eyes kind and strangely tolerant. ''As I recall, Quinn usually gets the girl in the final scene,'' he said meaningfully.

Her pale brown eyes glared at him. ''You'll never get me!''

He was looking past her shoulder at something. ''Won't I, Dana?'' he asked absently.

His hand left her waist to move caressingly against her throat. He lowered his head, herding hers back against his shoulder while his breath made a warm wind at her lips.

''Adrian…'' she whispered, starting to protest.

''They're not paying attention to us,'' he murmured, and his mouth opened to brush slowly across hers. ''Do you like this?'' he whispered seductively.

''Devil!'' she moaned.

''Yes,'' he whispered, coaxing her lips to follow his.

"Heartless...devil!"

"Yes, honey, yes," he murmured, his breath making chills against her moist lips.

"Adrian...!"

And something flashed as she hung there, her lips open and pleading as his met them briefly, open and demanding. Flashed, making her jump, breaking the spell, bruising her heart. A camera... somewhere.

She drew back, aware of smiling, teasing glances that caused her to blush. Without a word, she turned and went inside.

Adrian was two steps behind her. Her caught her hand again and locked her fingers with his.

"What's the matter?" he asked.

"Those people...staring," she muttered.

He only chuckled. "Things were getting interesting. I can make you burn without even trying, little girl."

She blushed furiously, without a comeback.

He squeezed her hand. "You didn't see the man with the camera, did you?"

She glanced up and the look in his eyes

puzzled her. There was something like triumph there.

"I...saw the flash," she admitted.

"It was one of the men from my personnel department. We have a company magazine," he told her. "You know, Mary on the shirt line is keeping company with Johnny in the Cutting Room...that kind of thing. I don't doubt that picture will make its way back to your friend Pat."

She felt all the color leave her face. "You saw the photographer coming, you did that to me deliberately...."

His eyes narrowed, glittered. "Damned straight," he said. "It's going to be interesting to hear you talk your way out of that."

"I'll simply tell him the truth," she shot back. "He'll believe me."

Sure enough, Pat was standing on the front steps Sunday afternoon with a brown envelope in his hand, and she knew what was in it by the look on his pale face.

She invited him into the living room, hoping against hope that Adrian wouldn't come downstairs.

Pat handed her the envelope without a word and she opened it. The picture was in glorious color. It shoved a dark, striking man with a slender blond girl in his arms, her hands gripping his powerful shoulders tightly as her lips touched his—open and pleading, her face a study in abject worship.

She closed her eyes and handed it back to him.

"Revealing, isn't it?" Pat asked quietly. "I don't have any strings on you, and I probably shouldn't be here at all. But you told me he was your boss and nothing more, and this picture makes a liar out of you. I'd just like to know the truth before we go any further together."

She stared down into her lap at her long, graceful hands. "He's a charming man, and he knows how to use that charm to his advantage. He set me up for that photo."

"There's nothing between you, then?" Pat asked gently.

"That," Adrian Devereaux said from the doorway, "is a matter of opinion."

Pat stood up quickly, his eyes taking in

the somber lines of her employer's face. "I know I'm here without permission. But I had to know," he explained, waving the brown envelope aimlessly.

"There's a simpler way," Adrian said. He paused to light a cigarette and pocketed his lighter, blowing out a thin cloud of smoke, eyeing Dana's apprehensive expression. "Ask her," he challenged Pat, "if she's ever slept with me."

Dana's face went white. Like plaster. Like sheetrock. Like a blank page.

Pat's jaw clamped harshly, his eyes hurt and contemptuous on the woman's face. "I don't have to ask her," he growled. "It's written all over her face! Dana, you little…!"

"Say it," Devereaux dared him, his eyes slits of brown flame, "and I'll break every bone in your body."

Pat's flush of anger left him abruptly as he saw the confidence in that leonine face and realized that Devereaux wasn't making an idle threat.

He tossed the brown envelope on the

sofa, and, without another word, turned and went out the door.

Adrian picked up the envelope and took out the photograph, his eyes taking on a soft, dark warmth as he studied the two figures in it.

"I think I'll have it framed," he said carelessly.

"It will remind you of me, won't you hate that?" Her voice broke, trembling. "Damn you, I cared about him!"

Something exploded in his face, in his eyes, in the hands that caught her shoulders and jerked her to her feet.

"What the hell do you know about caring?" he demanded. "If I cut you, you'd bleed printer's ink! You wouldn't know what to do with an honest emotion, you little zombie. My God, the only time I've ever seen you feel outside of a nightmare was when your mother died. And that softening didn't last long. Two days later, you were cased in ice!"

"You don't know what I feel or don't feel," she argued weakly, struggling to escape the merciless grip he had on her shoulders.

"The hell I don't," he growled. His blazing eyes met hers, the contempt in them dark and haunting. "You walked into my life in disguise, Meredith. You took everything there was to take and walked away without even looking back. I hated you for that, little girl, did you know? Not an apology, not a card, not a note or a phone call—nothing to tell me you cared one way or the other that you'd ruined me!"

"But, I tried…!"

"Not very hard, did you?" he demanded, his voice painfully soft with fury. "Three years I wondered if you could feel at all, and I saw that damned photo of you in that magazine, and I decided that, by God, I was going to teach you a lesson. Look here, Miss Meredith," he said, grabbing up the photograph to hold it under her wide, frightened eyes. "Look at the woman in this photograph! Her eyes soft and her mouth hungry, emotion in every line of her body. Not a trace of resemblance to the blonde zombie in that magazine I saw. This woman feels!''

She bit her lip to stop its trembling. ''And that makes you very happy, doesn't it, because if I can feel I can be hurt? Congratulations,'' she whispered. ''You've hurt me more than you'll ever know, and I hope you enjoy the triumph.''

His eyes darkened. ''Dana...''

''Pat was special to me,'' she continued, unable to stop now. ''He understood me, because he was like me—he knew what I meant when I talked about newspapers and reporting because it had been his life, too. When did you ever really talk to me? When did you ever do anything except hurt me?!''

He was looking down at her with a furrowed brow, his lips parted as if he was about to speak and couldn't get the words out.

''You said the name Persephone suited me and you were right because it's been hell living here with you!'' she cried brokenly.

His face became set, carved out of

stone, ashen under its tan. He let her go with a jerk. "Pack your bags and get out." He said it calmly, without raising his voice, but the words cut like a whip.

Her life changed in that space of seconds, and she stood there gaping at him. She'd planned things to do tomorrow, and now she wouldn't be here to do them, and it was like having her roots torn out from under her and tossed into a river.

"Now?" she whispered incredulously.

"Now. This minute. Get out, damn you!" he threw at her, his voice so harsh that she jumped.

Without another word, she turned and ran from the room. He was letting her go. Sending her away. And she knew that this time, there'd be no coming back. This time it was forever. Tears were washing her face when she reached her room.

Minutes later, she was packed. She called a cab, picked up her bag and purse and went hesitantly down the stairs, her steps light, as if any minute she expected him to come out and attack her.

"It's all right," Lillian said gently from the bottom of the steps. "He's gone out."

Dana's lower lips trembled with hurt and indignation. "He...fired me," she whispered.

"I heard," Lillian said with a sigh. "So did the neighbors, I'll wager—that last bit, anyway. Oh, honey, I'm so sorry. I just don't know what's wrong with that man lately!"

Dana stared down at her shoes. "He hates me," she said quietly. "I think he always has, he almost said as much to-day."

"And you love that man until it hurts, don't you, honey?" Lillian asked with a quiet knowing smile, watching Dana's face jerk up, astonishment in the soft brown eyes. "You light up like a Christmas tree when he walks into a room. You did three years ago. He didn't see it then, and he won't let himself see it now, either. But it's hard for a woman to miss."

Dana blinked away a rush of tears and bit her lower lip. "Look after my successor," she said in a husky voice. "He does yell. And…and don't forget to remind him about the…the Lions Club meeting next Tuesday, they're giving him a plaque for working in the conservation fund drive.'' Her voice broke. ''Damn him…!''

Lillian hugged her, hard, and took out a handkerchief to press into her small hand. ''Write to me,'' she said in a hoarse whisper.

Dana nodded through the tears. ''Bye.''

''Bye, honey.''

She lifted her case and went through the door just as the taxi pulled up at the steps. And she never looked back. Not once.

Sitting on the plane, her eyes red and burning, she fought down waves of anguish and forced her mind to concentrate on practical matters.

Money was the biggest problem. She had precious little left over from the plane fare. But, with luck, it would do her until she got her first paycheck.

She frowned in concentration and her plans began to jell. When she got to the airport, she'd get a taxi directly to the

newspaper office. First she'd see Jack and
get her old job back. Then she'd see about
an apartment or, in desperation, a motel
room until she could do better. Then, she'd
have something to eat. She'd skipped
breakfast, and there hadn't been time to eat
dinner...

She ignored the rumbling of her stomach, and closed her eyes on her future. A
tiny smile touched her mouth. It would all
work out.

If the dream was perfect, the reality cer-
tainly wasn't. Things started going wrong
the minute she got off the plane. To begin
with, she was in the cab headed for the
newspaper when it suddenly dawned on
her what day it was. Jack had Sundays off,
and could only be found out on a boat
somewhere in the Atlantic. That threw everything off schedule. So she had the cab
turn around and take her back to the room-
ing house she'd boarded in weeks ago.

Her old room was taken, and there was
nothing else available. She didn't have a
newspaper to look for apartments in, and

counting the substantial fee she already owed the taxi, her meager savings were hardly enough to cover two days' lodging in a motel now. With a sigh, she had the driver drop her off at a downtown motel.

Meals at those prices were going to be impossible, she saw that immediately. There was a small grocery store down the street, and she hoped it kept convenient store hours as she walked wearily toward it. Her eyes were drawn to the palm trees, her nose tickled by the sea smell of the nearby ocean. She drew in a deep breath. Part of her had missed this tropical atmosphere, missed the sand and the sea and the rough-barked palms waving in the wind on their crooked, curved trunks. It was only when she thought of Adrian that the pain came, the hurt. It was like having one part of her missing, like being half a person, without him. But then, she reminded herself, it had been this way three years ago and she had lived through it then. She'd live through this, too.

The store, mercifully, was open, and she brought a loaf of bread and a can of sandwich spread and a couple of soft drinks from a smiling old man whose accent was decidedly Cuban.

"Muchas gracias," he grinned as she paid him. *"Tiene usted...*excuse me, I speak English, your face is known to me, Senorita. You work near here?"

She studied him, frowning. His face, too, was familiar...

"Esteban," she recalled, smiling. "Esteban Valdez. I interviewed your son—he was one of the refugees on that last boatload..."

"Yes, my son, Jorge," he laughed. "He now has a job, many thanks to the fine story you wrote about him."

She felt the warmth steal up into her cold heart and warm it. Her eyes crinkled with pleasure. "I'm so glad."

"You are still a reporter?" he asked her.

"So far, I'm a tourist," she laughed. "I hope to go back to work for the paper. I've...been away for a while."

"Well, I hope it goes well with you. Say, you like *planatos fritos*?"

Her high school Spanish failed her. "What?" she asked.

"Ah…fried bananas," he grinned.

"I don't know, I've never tried them."

"Maria, she want to meet you, to thank you for the story about Jorge before, but at the paper they couldn't tell us where you were," he apologized. "Tomorrow, you come home with me for dinner, and Maria make for you *arros con pollo*—you know, chicken with rice!"

The friendly openness of the invitation was sunshine after a storm. "If I'm free tomorrow, I'd love it. Maria won't mind?"

"My wife is a good woman," he replied. "And a very good cook. Twelve o'clock tomorrow. You remember."

"Oh, I'll remember for chicken and rice," she said.

Esteban had cheered her up. But the lonely motel room had just the opposite effect. She slept fitfully, her stubborn mind going forever back to that parting scene with Adrian, feeling the anger and the hurt flood her heart all over again. Part of her could hate him, but the other part loved him too much to maintain that hatred. She forced his dark face to the back of her mind. She had to erase him from her life, to begin to learn how to live without him. Tomorrow she'd have a job, and everything would be fine.

When she got to Jack's office first thing the next morning, another disaster befell her.

"Oh, hell, Dana, why didn't you come Friday?" Jack growled, pacing the floor of his office. "It's all my fault, I was holding the job open—but I talked with Devereaux last week, and he gave me the idea that...well, that you weren't coming back. I'm sorry. I filled the slot Friday, and it was the only reporting job I had."

She felt the floor drop out from under her, thinking of how little money she had, and how much more it would take to live. She took a deep breath to keep from passing out.

"There was a job in composing," Jack sighed. "We filled that Saturday. God, I'm sorry! Dana, look, if you need any money..."

She shook her head proudly and managed a smile. "No, uh, I have all I need." She stood up. "Jack, thanks anyway."

"What for?" he growled, self-contempt in every word. "For selling you out?" He sighed heavily. "I hope I'm doing the right thing," he muttered and glanced at her. "Where are you staying?"

She told him, puzzled at his strange behavior.

He jotted it down. "I'll look around and if I find anything, here or on another paper, I'll call you. Going to be there for another day or so?"

"Probably," she said, noncommittally.

"Don't worry," he said, gazing at her pale, haunted face. "Everything's going to be all right."

"Is it?" she thought bitterly. But she only smiled and said, "Sure."

Sitting over a cup of steaming black coffee after the delicious meal at Esteban's, she sighed and forgot the hopelessness of the future. So she starved! This meal would go a long way.

"Good, huh?" Maria grinned, as big as her husband was thin. "Eat more."

Dana shook her head. "I can't. But thank you so much, it was delicious, all of it!"

Esteban studied her with narrowed eyes. "Miss Meredith...Dana, if I may... something is wrong, I can tell. Please, you helped my son, is there some way we can help you?"

Dana sighed with a tiny smile. "Only if you can pull a job out of a hat. The newspaper doesn't need me."

There was a rapid exchange of Spanish as Maria and Esteban discussed the situation.

"Does it matter what you do?" Esteban asked quickly. "I mean...Maria knows where there is a job, but it is not so...I mean, you may not want to..."

"Esteban, I have sixteen dollars in my purse," she told him with quiet pride. "And a very expensive bracelet which I'd rather starve than pawn. Does that answer your question? I don't have time to go to an employment agency or the labor department and wade through prospective jobs that will probably be filled when I get there. I'll gladly wait tables, wash dishes, or scrub floors...anything so that I can eat and keep a roof over my head. That's my only immediate ambition.''

"Spoken like a true...what is the word, *trooper*?" he grinned. "*Si*, it is waiting tables in a small cafe. Hard work and long hours, but the tips will be good. Can you go now with Maria to see?"

She nodded. "Esteban, how do I thank you, both of you?" she asked earnestly.

"Repeat after me, *muchas gracias*," he laughed.

It wasn't much of a cafe. The paint was peeling off the walls, there were rips in the vinyl seats of the booths, and occasionally an ant made a pilgrimage across the scarred tile floor. But Cherry Johnson, who owned the restaurant, paid good wages and kept out drunks and took Dana under her wing as if she'd been a baby chick. And Dana began to enjoy the routine, to recognize certain customers as regulars, to look forward to a job without the kind of pressures that had dominated her young life. Maria had helped her find a small, clean apartment just a block from the cafe, and one of the regular latenight customers, an elderly man, escorted her home to see that she got there safely.

She had everything she needed, Dana told herself. She felt a twinge of guilt about leaving the motel without a forwarding address, and about not getting back in touch with Jack, but what was the use?

A week after she took the job, Cherry Johnson sold the cafe to a stiff-necked ex-bartender who began an immediate renovation of it and rode Dana from dawn until dusk about trifles. What had begun as a pleasant job rapidly turned into a nightmare and she had no way out. The tips were too good, and she earned as much in one night as she might have in two days on the paper. It was better to put up with the abuse and the criticism and eat than to walk out and be in the frightening position she'd found herself in before. She gritted her teeth, and worked even harder, and pretended that she was about to embark on a protracted cruise to Tahiti.

But it was telling on her. She'd lost weight—it was inevitable since she had little appetite. Her face was pale and drawn, her eyes wide and haunted in that thin wanness, her whole look one of mute resignation. The long hours were tiring, her legs ached at night. And in her dreams, Adrian came to haunt her like a handsome dark ghost.

The bracelet stayed tucked away in a bureau drawer, carefully hidden, and sometimes she took it out and just looked at it. This morning, she wore it under her longsleeved blouse. It was precious, because he'd given it to her. Ironically, the amount she could have sold it for would have solved all her problems. But she'd honestly have starved rather than sell it.

It was the longest day she could remember, and she felt weak from the effects of lifting and carrying heavy chairs. Sanders, her new boss, had her shift tables around because he didn't like the setup.

"Stop loafing, Dana," he whined when

she paused to lean heavily on a chair, her face almost white with weariness, the reddish light of the sunset filtering through the window to tinge her hair with fiery glow.

"I'm not loafing, Mr. Sanders," she said quietly. "I'm so tired…"

"I thought reporters were on the move all the time," he chided, folding his fleshy arms to study her with his tiny black eyes. "That's what you were, right? One of them nosey reporters. I hate reporters, Miss Meredith, did you know that?"

"Yes, sir," she replied.

"Fancy lady," he growled distastefully. "All mind, no brawn. I got half a mind to kick you out in the… Well, now, what's that? The clientele is definitely improving! Get up off that chair, you cow, here comes a customer!" he snapped at Dana.

The bell on the door jingled as it opened. "Yes, sir, what can we do for you?" Sanders asked with a grin.

A tingling sensation in the back of Dana's neck made her straighten and turn around. And a surge of feeling, like hundreds of volts of electricity, ran through her body like sunlight filtering through satin. Adrian!

The shock of seeing him, of having him see her in such a deplorable state, brought tears to her eyes. She stood there gaping at him in a burning silence, her hair hanging half up, half down, her face white and drawn, her eyes red-rimmed, her cap sliding sideways on her head, her uniform crumpled... Miniature explosions were taking place in the dark eyes that ate her from head to toe.

Without a word, he moved toward her, stopping only inches away. He removed the cap from her head with meticulous care, studied it as if it were some strange insect. Then, with a contempt that said more than words ever could, he dropped it on the floor and ground it under his polished shoe.

''Hey, you can't do...'' Sanders began angrily.

Adrian turned and looked at him. That was all, but it must have been enough, because the man turned and went into the kitchen.

"Let's go," Adrian told her in a voice like none she'd ever heard, as if he were choking, strangling, with fury.

He caught her hand, ignoring the tears streaming down her cheeks, and half led, half dragged her out of the cafe to the waiting gray Rolls with Frank at the wheel. He put her inside and got in after her, drawing the curtain between them and Frank as he told the driver in a voice like shredded ice to drive around the city.

The car pulled away from the curb, and Adrian turned toward her, his eyes as dark as singed chestnuts, his face ashen under the tan, his jaw taut, his mouth a thin line. And with a groan almost of anguish, he reached for her.

Wrapped in those big, warm arms, she let the tears come, let the sobs shake her slender body. It was like coming home. He rocked her gently, his face buried in the tangle of hair at her throat, his strong fingers like pegs digging into her back as he bruised her against him. Incredibly, he was trembling; his breathing as harsh and ragged as if he'd been running.

"Dana," he whispered hoarsely, his breath warm against her neck through the silky hair. "Oh, God, honey…!"

"I love you," she whispered brokenly, her hands warming against the broad chest where her cheek was pressed. "Adrian, I love you so, I love you…"

He stiffened. Froze. She could feel every separate muscle of that massive chest contract as if he'd been struck by a bullet.

She caught her breath and closed her eyes on the humiliation that came after that involuntary outburst. "I'm sorry," she whispered. "That just…just slipped out. Please let me go…"

"Never." The word was spoken in such a low tone, and so huskily, that she barely heard it. His big arms contracted until they hurt her, and it was the sweetest pain she'd ever known. "I'll never let you go, not as long as I live…here, Dana…" He tilted her face just a little, and his mouth went down against hers, warm and hard and almost terrifyingly hungry. She felt a tremor rip through him, felt the sudden harsh intake of breath, felt his hard mouth opening sensuously against hers. With a tiny cry, she gave him back the bruising kiss, and the heavens seemed to burst with color behind her closed eyelids. Dazed with the force of her own response, she vaguely heard him as he murmured, ''Baby, I love you,'' fiercely against her mouth, over and over again. Out of a nightmare had come the wonder of paradise.

Minutes later, they were sitting quietly in a well-lit supermarket parking lot while cars and shoppers came and went around them with intense curiosity.

''We're being stared at,'' Dana murmured, her cheek resting comfortably against the warm white silk of Adrian's shirt, the heavy comforting beat of his heart at her ear.

''Let them stare,'' he murmured back, brushing a lazy kiss across her forehead. ''Dana, do you know how long I've been looking for you? Do you know what I've been through not knowing where you were, or what you were doing...damn it, why didn't you call Jack and tell him you'd moved?!''

She drew back. "You knew!"

He made a disgusted face. "Oh, hell, of course I knew. You only had one place to go, and that was to him. I was on the phone before your plane even landed. I told him not to hire you, but to find out where you were staying and call me." He sighed wearily. "By the time I got here, with the usual aggravating obstacles like late flights and fouled up arrangements, you'd already left the motel. I've gone through two agencies of private detectives. They only found you this afternoon." He shook his head. "I had every jeweler in Miami and every pawn shop alerted. I thought you might pawn the bracelet and I'd find you through it.''

She unbuttoned her sleeve and raised her wrist under his astonished eyes. "You gave it to me," she explained gently. "I'd have sold one of my legs before I'd have given it up.''

His dark face tautened to steel with that admission, a muscle in his jaw working with the force of his emotions as he met her loving eyes. "I feel just that way about you, and that's God's own truth. You're so much a part of me, I think I'd die if I had to spend my life away from you. Is it that way with you?"

"Yes, Adrian. It was that way with me three years ago," she whispered tearfully.

His mouth touched hers so gently, so tenderly, it brought tears brimming over her eyelids. "I didn't realize until I'd thrown you out that first time, so long ago, that you'd taken half my soul with you. By the time I realized it, it was too late. Then, a few weeks ago, I saw your picture in the magazine, and all the love came flooding back, and I had to have one more chance," he whispered. "Just one more...and I couldn't seem to keep Fayre and Melbourne at bay long enough to find out how you really felt. I knew I could make you respond in a physical sense, I saw how you reacted to me. But it wasn't until that night in the kitchen when you asked me if I'd ever wanted children that I began to hope."

She gazed up into his eyes quietly. "That night...when you left me at the lake..."

"Wanting you until it hurt," he grinned, "and so jealous of Melbourne I could taste it...God I've never been so drunk in my life. I wound up at Fayre's apartment, without even realizing how I got there. She saw a golden opportunity and took me home for you to find. The irony of it," he mused with a long, meaningful glance at Dana's rapt face, "is that I haven't touched Fayre since you walked back into my life. I haven't wanted anyone but you."

The tears came back and she reached up to touch his face, letting her fingers explore his hard jaw, his mouth. "Pat was a friend, and just that, Adrian."

"I know. Jealousy can drive a man mad, little girl." He studied her. "Seventeen years, Dana..."

"I love you," she whispered. "I want to spend the rest of my life with you. I want to give you children and laughter and moonlight and unicorns..."

He swallowed heavily. "It might be a good idea if you married me before we start on the children," he suggested, with a wry smile.

She flushed sweetly. "If you say so. After all," she added, lifting her mouth to his, "you're the boss!"

*   *   *   *   *

SILHOUETTE *Romance*

Escape to a place where a kiss is still a kiss...
Feel the breathless connection...
Fall in love as though it were
the very first time...
Experience the power of love!

Come to where favorite authors—such as
**Diana Palmer, Stella Bagwell,
Marie Ferrarella** and many more—
deliver heart-warming romance and genuine
emotion, time after time after time....

*Silhouette Romance—
stories straight from the heart!*

Silhouette®
Where love comes alive™

Where love comes alive™

From first love to forever, these love stories are
for today's woman with traditional values.

A highly passionate, emotionally powerful
and always provocative read.

SPECIAL EDITION™

Emotional, compelling stories that capture the
intensity of living, loving and creating a family in
today's world.

INTIMATE MOMENTS™

A roller-coaster read that delivers romantic thrills
in a world of suspense, adventure and more.